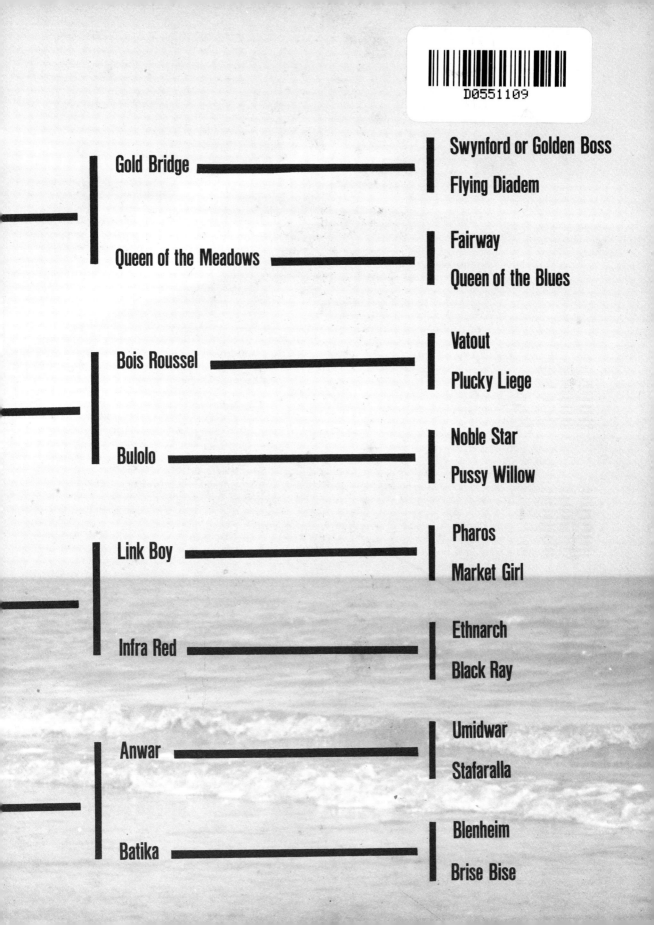

Gold Bridge ———————— | Swynford or Golden Boss
| Flying Diadem

Queen of the Meadows ———————— | Fairway
| Queen of the Blues

Bois Roussel ———————— | Vatout
| Plucky Liege

Bulolo ———————— | Noble Star
| Pussy Willow

Link Boy ———————— | Pharos
| Market Girl

Infra Red ———————— | Ethnarch
| Black Ray

Anwar ———————— | Umidwar
| Stafaralla

Batika ———————— | Blenheim
| Brise Bise

BORN TO WIN
The Story of Red Rum

BORN TO WIN

The Story of Red Rum

by Christine Pemberton

ILLUSTRATIONS BY ERIC ROWE

HODDER AND STOUGHTON
LONDON   SYDNEY   AUCKLAND   TORONTO

Frontispiece: After the 1977 Grand National – Red Rum, Tommy Stack and 'Ginger' McCain.

British Library Cataloguing in Publication Data
Pemberton, Christine
   Born To Win.
   I. Title
   823'.9'1J   PZ7.P/

ISBN 0-340-23146-7

Contents

Acknowledgements

The Publishers are grateful to the BBC and to Peter O'Sullevan for permission to quote from their commentary on the 1973 Grand National, and to the following people and agencies for their help in providing photographs:

Holden (Photographics) Ltd: 2, 13, 49, 65, 72, 103, 124, 125.
Carol Wareing: 25 (below).
The Huddersfield Examiner: 25 (top).
Keystone Press: 45 (top), 58, 68, 74.
Press Association: 45 (below), 115.
Sport and General: 51, 63.
Sporting Pictures (UK) Ltd: 31, 85.
Syndication International: 76.

Introduction

I first began to dream of training a horse to run in the Grand National when I was a boy. Why the National? Well, it's the most difficult and gruelling race of the English season, and the toughest challenge in racing. Many hard, disappointing years passed before I got my horse.

When I bought Red Rum on behalf of Mr Le Mare, whose own lifelong ambition had been to own a horse capable of running in the National, neither of us knew that Red Rum was going to fulfil our hopes beyond our wildest dreams. He won his first National by inches, his second by yards. Then he came second, twice. When, in 1977, he came back and won yet again, he became the only triple winner ever.

He quickly became part of the family, and his character has continued to grow with his fame. He knows that he is a hero and loves his public just as much as they adore him. Someone once said that the story of Red Rum was like a fairy tale. Everything that could have gone wrong did, but it all came out right in the end. There wasn't any magic involved, though. Just lots of courage, determination and hard work, plus a little bit of luck.

This is a story well worth telling. I know Red Rum would have told it to you himself, if he could. I am sure he has told Andy . . . And, when you read this book, you will agree that he deserves every bit of the success he so obviously enjoys.

Don McCain

Donald McCain.

Chapter One

THE INTRUDER

Andy knew from the start that this was no ordinary morning. He kept his nose down and carried on grazing, but his enormous long ears missed nothing and he kept one eye firmly on Mrs Wareing as she walked round the paddock, carefully checking the fencing yet again.

One of the children came running out of the bungalow. 'They've just telephoned, Mum. He's on his way,' he shouted.

Mrs Wareing patted the small grey donkey on the neck. 'I do hope that Andy gets on with him,' she said.

'Of course he will, Mum, he'll enjoy the company.'

'Humph,' thought Andy, nibbling furiously at the grass and pretending that he hadn't been listening. 'They'd better not bring another donkey here. This is *my* field. Company, indeed! I'll soon show him who's the boss, whoever he is.'

With a flick of his tail he trotted over to his favourite place, a dry, dusty patch he had made. He scraped up the dust with his front hooves and, when he was satisfied that it was sufficiently messy, sank happily into the clouds.

Company – who needed company? He rolled slowly on to his back and wiggled around for a moment, not the easiest of movements if you're a donkey. Then he waved his four legs at the sky, completed his roll and slowly got to his feet. He finished this performance by shaking vast quantities of dust into the morning air and returned to his grazing refreshed. There was nothing quite like a good old roll in the dust to make you feel on top of the world, he thought.

'Just look at him,' exclaimed Mrs Wareing. 'I spent ages brushing him and smartening him up last night. Now he's as bad as ever. I think he actually enjoys being scruffy.'

There was no time to do anything about Andy's scruffiness, though, for at that moment a large horse transporter, paintwork gleaming orange and cream, turned into the lane and stopped at the field gate.

Andy stared across the grass, quite forgetting that he had meant to ignore the actual arrival of his unwelcome companion.

'What sort of character is this?' he wondered to himself. Andy had been expecting a land-rover and trailer to turn up. A big, shiny transporter was far too grand for a donkey.

The driver and his companion began to let down the ramp, while Mrs Wareing opened the gate.

'Right, Billy,' called the driver. 'Lead him out.'

Andy, by this time, had wandered down the hedge and now stood in the corner, half hidden, his dusty grey blending with the shadows. He watched dumbfounded as Billy reappeared, leading the cause of all the fuss.

The horse paused at the top of the ramp, looking about him with a cool, regal confidence. The morning sunlight rippled off his gleaming coat, which was so fine that his veins stood out like a network of rivers and tributaries. His nostrils spread as he sniffed the fresh country air. Soft, over-large eyes took in the new surroundings in an instant and he tossed his fine, long head restlessly.

'Come on, Red,' said Billy quietly. 'Walk on.'

Slowly and grandly, the horse descended the ramp and Billy led him into Andy's field. Then Billy closed the gate, removed the halter and stood back.

Raising his head to the sky, Red sniffed again. Then he looked to each side of. the field, quickly measuring his boundaries, and a glorious sense of freedom flooded through him. The box had vanished, the track had gone and open field lay before him, filled only with the sweet smell of early summer grass.

His heart began to beat faster, his blood began to race with excitement. His legs, used to obeying instructions for so long, took charge. They flew over the grass, hooves thudding into the turf, and his tail rose out stiffly behind, beating time as he galloped.

Billy leant on the gate. 'He likes it,' he said, unnecessarily. Mrs Wareing cast an anxious glance at Andy, who was so nonplussed by this extraordinary performance in *his* field that he did not even pretend to graze. The horse circled the paddock joyfully, revelling in his wild gallop, and it was not until he thundered down the hedgerow for the second time that he noticed the small, shaggy donkey. He skidded to a sudden halt, his hooves tearing long marks into the turf as he did so. For a moment, the two stared at each other, and it was difficult to tell which was the more taken aback.

'This is my field,' thought Andy. 'It's about time I made that quite clear.'

He tossed his head, gave a wild slash at the air with his hind legs – a trick which seldom failed to impress – and set off on his own ungainly canter round his territory.

The new arrival watched this comical donkey-dance with interest for a minute, then decided to follow. Andy, who was putting on a fair turn of speed for a humble donkey, felt the earth shake with the thunder of hooves. A dark shadow appeared alongside his own, then it lay ahead of him and the horse flashed past.

Andy watched the rapidly vanishing tail with annoyance. There was, he decided, only one way to stop *that*. He halted, drew back his upper lip, and his sides began to heave. From deep within came a low grating, as if someone was sliding ancient, rusty bolts back and forth. The bolts gained speed and volume and were then overtaken by the sound of several tug boats sounding their horns together through an invisible fog. A few moments of silence followed and then the awful orchestra of old ironmongery began again.

The horse stopped in his tracks. He turned around and cantered back to the source of this dreadful racket. Andy stood his ground and repeated the performance.

'That's amazing,' said the horse. 'I wish I could do that, it would impress them at the racetrack.'

Andy, very pleased that his trick had worked, began to graze. 'The ability to bray,' he murmured smugly, crunching at the grass, 'is a privilege bestowed only upon the donkey.'

The horse lowered his head and pulled a delicious mouthful of young grass. 'Hmmm, that's very good.' He looked at the cocky little donkey. 'That may be so, just as the ability to win three Grand Nationals is a privilege bestowed only upon Red Rum.'

'They seem to have settled down together,' said Mrs Wareing.

'Your Andy'll not take any harm,' replied Billy. 'Red wouldn't hurt a soul.'

Mrs Wareing smiled. 'It wasn't Andy that I was worried about. It's such a responsibility, Red being here, and Andy can be a little devil. He's so possessive about that field. He doesn't like to share it.'

'Don't worry, Red can take care of himself,' Billy told her. ' You'll see, he's different, that one. A real gentleman, but he'll not stand any messing – look, see what I mean?'

Red was chasing Andy off and it was very obvious that the little donkey was no match for him. As they rounded the corner of the field, Andy ducked to one side and bolted into his tiny donkey shelter. Red cantered on along the hedge, slowing as he came round again towards Andy's sanctuary, and began to graze outside the entrance.

Andy's head appeared. 'Are you really Red Rum?'

The visitor raised his head from the grass. 'Yes, I am.'

Andy shuffled about inside the shelter. Finally he spoke. 'Well, I'm sorry if I was a bit – er – abrupt with you earlier, but this is *my* field, you know. What I'm trying to say is, well, er – you're welcome to share it but – er – do please try to remember that it *is* my field.'

Red put his head into the shelter. 'That's very nice of you, Andy. I've only come here for my summer holiday. I hope we can become

Red Rum jumping the water jump at Wetherby
with Ron Barry.

friends. By the way, please call me Rummie. That's what all my special friends do.'

Andy came out of the shelter and stood beside his new companion, who towered above him. 'Have you come far?' he asked, conversationally.

The horse wrinkled up his muzzle, displaying enormous, flat teeth, and flipped his upper lip back and forth, as if he were laughing.

Andy looked cross. 'I don't see what you find so funny, I was only trying to be friendly.'

Red looked down at the tetchy little donkey. 'Don't get mad, Andy. I wasn't laughing at you. It was what you said that amused me.'

Andy stamped a foot. 'If I can't get a civil answer to a simple question, I shall take no further interest in you, so there.'

'Calm down,' said Red, gently. 'Today I travelled only a very short distance to get to your paddock, but looking back down all my years, I must say that I have come a long way.'

He held his fine head high and gazed into the distance. His eyes had taken on a dreamy look and he seemed to have forgotten Andy. After a few minutes, the donkey nosed at his shoulder and the horse jumped.

'You were saying?' Andy was impatient. He had no time for day-dreamers.

Red began to crop the grass again. 'You set me thinking, Andy,' he replied, between lush mouthfuls. 'A great deal has happened to me, but it's so pleasant and peaceful here, it reminded me of another place, a long, long time ago.'

'You can tell me about it, if you like,' said Andy. 'It's a long time since I heard a story.'

'Well, if you're really interested, I will,' said Red.

Chapter Two

THE GYPSY FIELD

'My story begins far away from here, beyond the sea, in County Kilkenny which is in Ireland. I was born on the evening of May 3rd, 1965, at a place called the Rossenarra Stud, a special sort of farm where they breed lots of horses.

'I remember very little of my early months, except my mother, Mared. Mared was a real fiery character and she used to tell me such hair-raising tales about her early days that I began to wonder how she could be so kind and gentle towards me. To begin with, they tried to race her, but she wasn't having that. They'd get her to the racetrack and she'd start frothing and sweating and dancing about until she had built up a raging temper. Suddenly, away she'd go, so wild and fast that nobody could hold her. She had no self-discipline, my mother, and in the end they said she was mad. I think they just didn't understand her.'

'She sounds quite a character,' said Andy.

'Oh, she was, but she wasn't really bad, just very sensitive and she hated being *made* to do something. I'm the same. It is much nicer to do things because you really want to, that's something I discovered a long time ago. Anyway, they soon took my mother out of racing and she spent the rest of her time at the Rossenarra Stud as a brood mare. That suited her, I think. She seemed to enjoy rearing foals.

'My father was completely different, a cool grey named Quorum. He was as calm as Mared was fiery, and greatly respected. He was a fine sprinter, renowned for his stamina, and many of his sons have done well.

'There was another colt foal born at the Stud that year, and he became my first friend. In the autumn, we were turned out together into the Gypsy Field and there I had some of my happiest times. We were wild and carefree, fooling around together all day long, forever chasing and bucking at each other.

'In the evenings, when dusk fell, we grew calm, for that field was very special. Long ago, the gypsy people used to pull in there with their caravans. They would stay for a few days before they set off again on their roamings, and people said that they left good luck behind them. There was certainly something. At night we could feel it. There was a peaceful, happy quality in the air. Nothing you could see or touch, but it was there all right.

'We passed several happy months in the Gypsy Field, nearly a year, and then, one day towards the end of the summer, they took us up to the stables. It took a lot of getting used to, being confined like that after we had enjoyed such wild freedom.'

Rummie glanced over at Andy, who had been listening intently. 'You wouldn't understand, Andy, living out of doors and just pleasing yourself all the time. I expect you take this sort of life for granted.'

'For me,' replied Andy, 'this is the only sort of life. The shelter is nice enough when it's raining cats and dogs across the field, and it's fine to have a place to cool off in on a hot afternoon, when the flies won't leave you alone, but I only go into it when I choose. I'd be pretty annoyed if anyone tried to shut me up in there.'

Rummie nuzzled the donkey affectionately. 'I know exactly how you feel, Andy. Believe me, we felt even worse about it at first, being so young and restless, but I gradually began to realise that there was to be more to life for me than the carefree tomfoolery we had enjoyed in the Gypsy Field.

We had a great deal of learning to do. They began by getting us used to being handled. Each day, the grooms would take us, in halters, and walk us round and round. It was terribly boring and to begin with I tried to get away from them, but gradually I learnt to obey the gentlest of pulls on the halter as we were guided in different directions. I think they were rather relieved to find that I was better behaved than my mother. Like any frisky young yearling, I had my occasional high spirits, but nothing like the sweating hot tempers she had told me about.

One Monday, after our usual exercise period, the grooms spent a great deal of time with us yearlings, checking us over and grooming us more vigorously than usual. There were six of us. Something, we felt sure, was about to happen, and there was a great deal of talk and guessing that evening. Word travelled down the line, from box to box.

"We are being sent to a sale," said the young filly next to me. "I heard the men talking. They are taking us to the auction at Dublin."

I spent most of that night wondering what was going to happen to me. Who would buy me? Where would I go? I was excited, but also a little worried and sad. I knew that once I had left Rossenarra I would never come back, and I had been happy here. Would the next place be even better? I was eager to find out.

Early the next morning, the six of us were loaded into the horse-box and driven to Dublin. The noise of the traffic and the awful swaying of the vehicle were frightening.

I did not like the auction. There were a lot of horses there, all nervous and worried, and the grey, wet morning had put even the men in low spirits. Several came to look at me while I waited in a box for my number to be called.

As my turn drew closer, I grew increasingly tense and edgy, and, when one of the grooms came to lead me out, I went forward with such a rush that I slipped and hurt my leg. As they led me into the parade ring, I walked a bit stiffly and that, I think, stopped some people bidding for me. They thought I might be going lame.

I hated being led in circles around that miserable ring, with the faces of the crowd all blurred together, but the ordeal was soon over, for only two men were bidding. The auctioneer banged the table with his mallet and for four hundred guineas I was sold. As they led me out, I passed the young filly who had travelled with me. She was waiting to go into the ring.

"Good luck," she whinnied.

"Goodbye," I said, thinking that I should never see her again.

The next few hours were horrible, a nerve-racking time spent travelling. Together with several others, I was loaded into another horse truck and taken to the docks. When they led me out towards the gangplank, I sniffed sadly at the free air around me. For the first time I could smell the sea – a sharp tang and the taste of salt on my nose. I didn't know then how much that smell would come to mean to me later. The strange freshness of it lifted my flagging spirits. I suddenly realised, as they led me on board, that I was at the beginning of my journey, my long voyage far beyond the boundaries of Rossenarra. Who knew what lay ahead?

It was not until we were out at sea that I began to take much interest in my surroundings. With surprise and delight I realised that my young filly friend was also travelling with us.

"We are going to England," she informed me. "Maybe we will meet there. I am to be called Curlicue. A pretty name, don't you think?"

"Curlicue," I repeated. "I won't forget you. I can't tell you my name, Curlicue, because I don't yet have one."

That first long journey finally ended in Leicestershire, in the village of Wymondham. I was led out of my horse-box into a pleasant, tree-lined yard. On two sides of the yard were stables and at the far end stood the house where my new trainer, Mr Molony, and his family lived. I was taken to a box and left to enjoy peace and quiet, for the first time since I had set out from Rossenarra.'

Chapter Three

MY FIRST RACE

Andy had been so engrossed in Rummie's story that he had not noticed Mrs Wareing at the fence.

'Just look at that,' she said. 'It's incredible. I've never known Andy miss a carrot. He's usually here before I am.'

Rummie turned at the sound of her voice. 'I'm off now, Andy. Billy's come to get me and he'll have a pocket full of mints. I can never resist the things, and well he knows it.'

'Hang on a minute,' said Andy. 'I thought you said you were here for the rest of the summer.'

'I am, but they'll take me in at night. I'll be back first thing in the morning. Come on over with me, I think she's got a carrot for you.'

Andy followed Rummie to the gate. 'I don't know how you can bear to be shut up for the night,' he said. 'You don't realise what you're missing. These warm summer evenings are the best part of the day.'

'I'm used to it, Andy. Don't tempt me now, it's donkey's years since I spent a night in the open. You'll be able to have your field to yourself again, anyway. I thought you'd be glad.'

Andy careered down the side of the fence, braying after the horse. 'Come back,' he called. 'Don't forget to come back, will you?' Suddenly, the field seemed very empty. He mooched around, sniffing at the place where they had spent most of their time. Odd to think that until this morning he had never met Rummie. Moodily, he wended his way over to his old patch, sank into the dust and rolled back and forth several times. That really felt good.

'Andy, come along – carrots,' called Mrs Wareing.

Andy ambled over.

'Do you like Red?' she asked, as he crunched away. 'I think you do, don't you?'

Andy continued to work his way through the carrots and said nothing.

The sun was well up the next morning when Rummie was brought back. Andy, who had been haunting the gate since first light, watched admiringly as he circled the field in a wild, ecstatic canter. Rummie whinnied to him as he flew past. 'Come on, Andy, join in. I'm free again.'

Such joy was infectious and Andy found himself winging along in the wake of his friend. Rummie paused until Andy had caught up with him, nuzzled him along his shaggy grey shoulder in greeting and was then overtaken by another explosion of energy which seemed to catapult him across the turf. Andy, fast realising that it was impossible to keep up with him, followed for a few moments at his own pace, before deciding that it would be more sensible to carry on grazing until Rummie's morning madness had worn itself out.

'I hope you feel better after that,' he said, when Rummie at last had had enough.

'Oh, Andy, it's almost worth being shut up for the night for the sheer joy of coming back on to grass. All I need now is a good roll, and then we'll get down to some serious grazing.'

He lay down on the grass, thrust his smooth, shining hooves towards the sky and rolled luxuriously from side to side, then right over. He stood up again and shook himself.

Andy, greatly amused to see such an important personage indulging in these capers, said, 'You're no different from the rest of us, really, are you?'

Rummie looked at him sharply. 'Did anyone say that I was?'

'Well, no,' admitted Andy. 'But you jockey-lovers . . . '

Before he had time to finish the sentence, Rummie, head down low and menacing, charged forward to see him off. Andy retreated hastily into the donkey shelter.

Rummie stamped angrily outside. 'Don't you *ever* call me that,' he bawled. 'How dare you insult me like that! You know *nothing*– d'you hear – *nothing!*'

'Heavens,' thought Andy, still inside the shelter. 'What have I said?' He peered nervously round the entrance. 'Don't take on so, Rummie. I only meant . . . '

'I know exactly what you meant,' shouted Rummie. 'And I won't have that said of me. You don't understand anything, you – you – *you Asshead.*'

'How rude,' thought Andy. He was sorely tempted to bray 'Jockey-lover' again through the doorway, but managed to stop himself.

A long, sulky silence followed, during which each began to feel rather guilty about his treatment of the other. Finally, Rummie peered into the shelter. 'Are you going to stay in there all day?'

'I might.'

'Come on, Andy. It's a fine, sunny morning and it would be a shame to spoil it by quarrelling.'

Andy poked his head out. 'Are you going to tell me some more about yourself?'

'Yes,' said Rummie. 'I think I'd better. It is very wrong of you to go around making assumptions about people, you know. Things are not always exactly as they may seem.'

Andy followed him across the field, and for a while they grazed in silence. Finally Andy spoke. 'What happened to you at Wymondham, Rummie?'

'Wymondham,' echoed Rummie. 'Well, looking back now, I suppose you could say that the things that I learnt there, and the way that I was taught them, were as important to me as anything that has happened since. I had to learn discipline and control – both very boring subjects when you're a fresh and leggy yearling. I took some of it pretty hard, as we all do, but I've spoken to many horses since those days, and I must say that I fell into good hands. They had the patience not to rush me, and I've had good cause to be grateful for that as the years have passed.

I can still remember the first violent shock of having a man up on my back. The worst part was not being able to see him. I could hear him breathing, way behind my ears, and the smell of him came drifting down to my nostrils. The weight and the pressure of him were frightening, and his legs straddled down against my sides.

To make matters worse, he was tense, just as I was, and I would have really gone crazy in my attempts to cast him off, except for two things. One was a small steel bar in my mouth, which I already knew from experience could be made to cause me a great deal of pain, pain that would only stop if I behaved as instructed. The other, even more important, was that Mr Molony stayed close by my head. He held me firmly and talked to me in such a quiet, soothing tone that my confidence began to return. As the days passed, I grew calmer, and before long I was going out on rides with the other horses.

It took me a long time to get used to traffic. I unseated my rider more than once, and the stable lads came to regard me as quite a challenge, but they all took it in good part and it became something of a joke in the yard, getting unseated by me.

One day, a few weeks after my arrival, a gentleman came down to the stables to look at me. Listening to the conversation outside my box, I realised that he was my owner.

"If he's going to the 'Seller' at Liverpool," said the gentleman, "it's time he had a name. Now let's see, he's out of Mared, by Quorum, so we want something that's a bit of both."

He rubbed his chin thoughtfully. "I've got it," he said suddenly. "Red Rum. It's got to be Red Rum." And that is how I got my name.

The 'Seller' at Liverpool was to be my first race and I was as excited about it as the men. For weeks beforehand, all my training was aimed at getting me really fit, building me up into the peak of condition, and I began to enjoy it. The more I worked, practising out on the gallops with the other horses, the more relaxed and confident I became, and Mr Molony was pleased with my progress.

I had better explain here that I was being trained to be a sprinter, to run in short, fast races on flat ground. The career of a sprinter begins early in life. You start racing before you're two years old and are usually past your best and ready to retire by the time you get to four.

The training of a potential steeplechaser, who will run farther and over jumps, is quite different. His working life doesn't begin much before the age of four. His early years are spent out at grass and he's left in peace until he's finished growing. I was unlucky. Since no one then had any inkling that there might be more to me than my pedigree indicated — that I was going to become a steeplechaser — those few months of freedom I had enjoyed in the Gypsy Field were to be the only ones I spent at grass throughout my youth.

Anyway, the big day came, and there I was, just six months after leaving Rossenarra, circling the paddock at Liverpool and waiting for my first race to begin. It was a fine April day, the sort of day when things happen, and the air was charged with excitement. I was in a fine mood, anxious to show what I could do.

We were just getting into position for the start when I spotted Curlicue, but before I had a chance to call to her, we were off. The surprise of seeing her had distracted me and I began more slowly than I had meant to. It took me a few moments to get back into my stride. The race itself was quite overwhelming. There were horses on every side and I found it difficult to concentrate. My jockey must have realised for he started thrusting me forward, and his instructions were coming so fast that I had no more time to wonder.

On and on we galloped and I felt myself beginning to tire. Then I saw Curlicue ahead of me. She was going like the wind and I wanted to catch her up. I forgot the tiredness and my legs gained a life of their own. It was a marvellous sensation, flying over the track, on and on until I was alongside my friend. We reached the winning line together – Curlicue and I had made it a dead heat.'

'Did she recognise you?' asked Andy.

'Not right away, until I reminded her. I had no name when we parted, and Red Rum had meant nothing to her in the paddock. Our paths never crossed again, but I did hear later that she had been bought back by Mr McEnery, our breeder. He took her back to Rossenarra as a brood mare. It was a strange coincidence, though, running against each other and finishing together in our very first race.

From then on, it was all work. I enjoyed it, but I did miss being out in the summer. As I travelled mile after mile, to yet another racetrack, I would sometimes glimpse a field and be filled with longing. There it lay, green and lush in the sunlight, so inviting that I could almost taste the young grass. I felt homesick for the Gypsy Field and I wanted to cast off the saddle and be free again. I ran in eight more races and experienced many changes of jockey, which never gave me the chance to get used to any of them, but I went on doing my best and finally, at the end of September, they retired me for the season.

I enjoyed my winter at Wymondham. Now that we had more time to relax, Mr Molony began teaching me to jump, which I enjoyed immensely. When spring came around again, I felt fresh and powerful and they entered me for an important race at Doncaster. I knew that I was favoured to win and I was determined not to let them down. It was a hard race, but I won by a head and it was not until later that I realised what my achievement meant.

The race I had just won was a 'Seller', which meant that, by the rules under which it was run, we all had to be offered for sale afterwards. The same thing had happened at Liverpool, but nobody had seriously wanted to buy me then. This time it was different. My joy in my triumph faded as I realised what was happening. Jock, from the stables, led me round the crowded ring.

"Don't worry, old son," he whispered. "Mr Molony'll not let you go. He's going to buy you back in."

This knowledge comforted me, but it soon became clear that I was now of far greater value than I had been when I first left Rossenarra. Someone in the great sea of faces was very anxious to have me. I felt Jock stiffen as the bidding rose beyond a thousand guineas.

"Someone's after you, all right," muttered Jock. "Mr Molony can't go on bidding for ever."

The auctioneer's gavel banged down. "Sold for fourteen hundred guineas," he announced.

Jock and I looked over at the rest of the lads from the yard.

"Bought in by Mr Molony," finished the auctioneer.

Jock and the other lads grinned as they led me through the crowd, back to my box. "Come on, Red, let's get you washed down. You're

Summer companions.
Andy, Mrs Wareing's daughter Jillian and Red Rum.

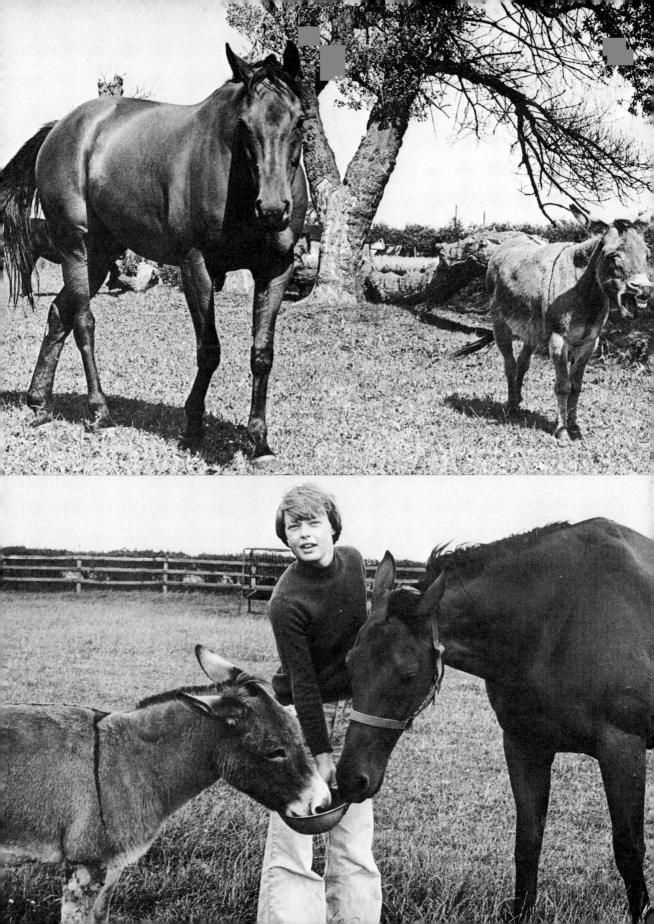

coming back home—I told you the Guv'nor wouldn't let you go, didn't I?''

At Wymondham, everyone was delighted to see me back, and Mr Molony began to plan my programme for the next season. By this time, I was jumping well, and he intended to send me hurdling. In the meantime, I was to be ridden by the famous Lester Piggott at Liverpool. I ran a marvellous race and everyone, including me, believed that I had just beaten my only rival at the winning post. My number flashed up on the winner's board, but we scarcely had time to rejoice before the loudspeakers announced that there had been a mistake, and that I was placed second. There was nothing that anyone could do about the decision, but I did hear Jock saying that, as far as he was concerned, I was the winner.

And that, Andy, was the end of my stay at Wymondham. Suddenly, I was in a horse-box, on my way to Yorkshire.'

'What ever happened?' asked Andy.

'It still makes me angry when I think about it. There was never any chance to look around and say goodbye to the lads. They just whisked me away, that's what happened. My owner had arranged it very quietly – he'd sold me to an old friend and rival – and they did not even know at the yard, which is why I had no inkling of it. It was not until I was in my new box at Oxclose that the realisation began to hit me, and I felt both sad and annoyed at being sneaked away like that.'

'I don't know how you put up with that sort of treatment,' said Andy. 'I wouldn't.' He pulled at the grass. 'And there's another thing. I've been thinking. You're on holiday, aren't you? You've worked hard all year – you've earned this break?'

'Of course I have.'

'Right. Then why do you keep going in like a lamb every evening? It's no fun at all, being stuck in that stable on a fine summer's night. Stay out with me. You should just taste the grass, first thing, when the dew is still on it. By the time they bring you out, the sun's dried it off. Just think of it, Rummie, you could run beneath the stars . . . Go on, Rummie, let's play up when they come for you. Stay out tonight.' The little donkey nuzzled Rummie's shoulder excitedly. 'Say you'll stay out with me.'

'It would be fun,' Rummie admitted. 'The trouble is, it's the mints.

Billy always has a pocketful when he comes for me, and I just can't resist them.'

'Of course you can,' said Andy crossly. 'There's more to life than mints, you know. Think of the grass with the dew still on it. You're on holiday, Rummie – you'll be back to peppermints and racetracks soon enough.'

'You're right, Andy. I'll do it. Poor Billy is going to get a bit of a surprise when he comes for me.'

Chapter Four

SANDRA

Billy tapped on the kitchen window and mouthed something through the glass.

'I can't hear you,' called Mrs Wareing. 'Just a minute.' She came to the door. Billy stood there, a halter dangling from his hand. 'Have you come to take Rummie back?'

Billy grinned. I did, but I can't catch him. Every time I get near, he just canters off with Andy. They're having some sort of game with me, I'm sure. I know it sounds crazy, but it's almost as if they'd plotted it between them.'

'Surely he'll come for a peppermint,' said Mrs Wareing.

Billy shook his head. 'Not even for a mint. It's the first time it's ever failed. I don't know what's got into him.'

'It must be Andy,' said Mrs Wareing. 'Oh dear, it looks as though he's going to be a bad influence on Red. I'd rather hoped that that donkey might learn a few manners, not the other way round.'

'Don't worry about it,' said Billy. 'We'll leave them out together. It won't do Red any harm. The change will be good for him. He'll be spending long enough in his box once he goes back into training. I'd better be getting back to the yard, now. I've plenty to do there.'

Billy climbed up into the empty transporter and glanced across the field. Rummie and Andy were grazing, nose to nose, like two conspirators. 'See you, Red,' he called.

Rummie looked up, a little shamefaced at his triumph, but Andy was so delighted that he raced down the fence after the retreating vehicle, braying loudly in a most cheeky fashion.

'That sorted your Billy out,' he gloated, returning to his grazing.

'Poor Billy, I do hope that he doesn't get told off,' Rummie worried. 'He's a good lad, my Billy.'

'For goodness' sake, stop worrying, will you? You're here to enjoy yourself.'

Being almost midsummer, the warm evening drifted endlessly, lazily towards nightfall. Rummie, standing with his back against the hedge, felt his eyes begin to close, and he dozed happily, enjoying the busy chattering of a family of hedge sparrows as they bustled their fledglings back to the nest. Way beneath, the grass rustled and a tiny fieldmouse scurried out from his hole. A long spiral of midges zig-zagged along on a warm current of air.

Andy wandered over, surprised and rather pleased to see this great powerhouse of restless energy so relaxed. 'Wake up, Rummie, it will be dark soon. The lights have already gone on in the bungalow. You don't want to miss the stars, do you?'

'Eh? Oh, Andy,' Rummie tossed his head, feeling rather embarrassed to have been caught napping.

Andy stood alongside him. 'I thought you were going to tell me about Oxclose. How long did you stay there?'

'A long time, Andy. Four years. At one time, I thought I would always be there.

'As I told you, I was hurt and annoyed when I realised what had happened and to begin with I behaved rather badly. It was a quiet place, quite unlike either of my previous homes. There were no children to play there and I missed seeing a family around the yard. No laughing, no shouting, nothing to keep me alert and interested when I looked out of the box.

'I felt fidgety and restless. I think that I would soon have grown as subdued as my surroundings, except for one thing.' Rummie paused, wondering whether he should say any more. He had never told anyone his private secret, and it was doubtful if Andy would understand.

'Go on,' Andy demanded. 'What thing?'

Rummie looked at the impatient little donkey. 'I don't know if I should tell you. You'd probably laugh, knowing you. I don't think you'd be able to understand.'

Andy was offended. 'You think a great deal of yourself, Red Rum. My life certainly lacks glamour, compared to yours, but there's no need to insult me. If you think your story is too complicated for my simple donkey mind, you'd better keep it to yourself.' He cantered away in a huff.

'Oh dear,' thought Rummie. 'Here we go again.' He followed Andy up the field to the shelter.

'Come on out, you silly moke,' he ordered. 'You've completely misunderstood me. I will tell you, but I warn you, you'll hurt me deeply if you laugh at me.'

Andy trotted out of the shelter with dignity. 'Go on, then. I'm listening.'

'Once I had got over feeling sulky about everything, I decided that, to begin with, at least, I would give whoever was to look after me a hard time. I felt rebellious and in no mood to give way to my new stable lad. I spent all that first homesick night planning what I would do. I could hardly wait for the morning, when the new lad turned up. I was going to play the very devil.'

'Quite right, too,' muttered Andy.

'Well, it took the wind right out of my sails when this young girl appeared. She came to my box and talked to me and then she led me out into the yard. When she tacked me up and got on, well, I was quite taken aback. Light as a feather, she was, and chatting away to me in such a soft, gentle voice that I felt I ought to behave for her. Then I remembered how annoyed I was, so I started dancing and bucking, but not as violently as I had intended. The girl seemed amused, almost

With Tommy Stack in the paddock
just before the 1977 Grand National.

pleased, by my spirited behaviour. She relaxed and stayed with me.

' "He's a devil," she called to the men who were watching us. "Marvellous horse – watch him go." '

'We bucked off across the field and suddenly I began to see the funny side of it. The more I played up, the more she loved it and soon we were winging away together, across the early morning, thoroughly enjoying ourselves. Sandra – that was her name – Sandra and I . . . ' he paused shyly.

'What are you trying to say?' asked Andy quietly.

'Something that I've never told another soul.'

'You can tell me,' said Andy. 'I do understand.'

Rummie looked at him. 'Then I don't need to say it, do I?'

'No, Rummie, I know what you mean.'

'That was the most important thing that had ever happened to me,' continued Rummie, 'The friendship between me and Sandra.'

He looked up and was overjoyed to see the dark, starry sky spreading out, everywhere he looked. He gave a small whinny of pleasure. 'I can't remember when I last saw the whole night sky, Andy. Look, it goes on for ever. All I ever see from my box is a narrow strip. I am glad that you persuaded me to stay out.'

'You were telling me about Sandra,' Andy reminded him.

'Sandra and I understood each other right from the beginning. There was no fooling her, as I'd planned. She knew when I was playing up – saw straight through me. Before long, she could do anything with me, because I hadn't the heart to make things difficult for her by misbehaving. I wouldn't put up with anyone else, though. I behaved so badly that no one else would ride me, which suited me, of course.

Sandra had me all the time, schooling me on and preparing me for the coming season. I enjoyed working with her and she was delighted with my progress. When they sent me down for my very first race over the hurdles, she travelled with me. I was really looking forward to that race, right up to the moment when she handed me over to the jockey. That's when I lost my confidence.

For weeks, no one but Sandra had ridden me. I had grown so used to her that I knew what she wanted me to do before she gave the order. It was a shock suddenly to have a stranger in the saddle again – and how he drove me! Any thoughts of misbehaviour that I may have harboured

were quickly dispelled. He had been warned that I might prove difficult to handle and it was clear that he did not intend to leave me any
margin. I was taken by surprise at the way he pushed me on, and I re-
sponded with reluctance. The silent battle of wills quickly exhausted
me and as we came towards the finish I began to slacken pace. To draw
the final effort from me, he began to use the whip. It wasn't the pain,
although that was bad enough – it was the degradation that really hurt
me. I felt so ashamed, as we ran on down that track to finish second.
Until then, I had enjoyed racing. Surely it didn't have to be like this?

When Sandra came to take me back to my box, I could see that she
was upset at the state I was in.

We set off back to Oxclose and I prayed that I might never see that
course again.

As it drew nearer, I began to dread my next race, for this time I was
afraid. I could not forget the misery of my previous experience. When
the day came, I began to sweat with nervousness as they led me round
the paddock. To begin with, I was relieved to find that I had a different
jockey, but this time the ground was too soft for my liking. I was so
terrified of slipping that I could not concentrate properly and this
jockey, sensing my lack of enthusiasm, began to urge me on. I quickened, but he was still not satisfied. I don't know which was worse – the
sting of the whip or the awful, slippery ground beneath me that I dared
not trust. All my pleasure in racing suddenly disintegrated. Now it just
meant pain and fear.

That night, Sandra came to me, in my box, and began to bathe those
ugly stripes that the whip had left. When she had finished, she came
round and held my head, stroking very softly down my nose.

"Rummie," she whispered. "My poor Rummie, how could they?"

There were tears in her eyes, Andy. She was as hurt as if they had
whipped her, too. I tried to comfort her, nuzzling against her. It was
wonderful to know that she cared so much and I could hardly bear to
see her so upset. That's when I decided to race as never before. I would
run for myself, Andy, and for Sandra, because it really mattered to her.
I still needed a jockey to help me, but I wasn't going to let anyone on
top get that powerful ever again. The way I was going to run, no one
would ever need to. I would practise and learn and build up my stamina
until I could go like the wind.'

'And did you?' asked Andy.

Rummie nodded. 'Oh yes, I did it all right. I won each one of my next three races and Sandra was delighted. But after that I was tired. I'd worked really hard for those achievements and it was time to rest me. I longed to go out to grass. From my box, I could see some of the other horses enjoying the freedom of the fields, and the sight of them almost drove me mad. It was three summers since I had left the Gypsy Field. Three summers since I had had any free time to myself. My heart wasn't in that next race, Andy. I'd had enough. I was crying out for the summer grass.'

'Did you get it?' asked Andy. Rummie's story had subdued him and he was wishing that he had been gentler towards the horse when he had arrived. Poor Rummie, no wonder he had danced for joy that first morning, when Billy had let him loose into the field.

'Yes, eventually they turned me out, but I'd missed the best of it. It wasn't young and sweet any more. I felt sad to realise that it would be another long year before the grass was new again. It wasn't just self-indulgence, Andy. I needed that young grass to restore me, to put back what the racing seasons had taken from me.

By the end of the winter I felt low and run down, and when the cough virus travelled through the stables, it hit me particularly hard. Every breath became a tiring effort, and I felt my strength lessening with each week that passed. They took me to the tracks fourteen times that year, and each time I failed to win. I had neither forgotten nor revoked the promise I had made to myself, but I just wasn't well. I had done too much too quickly. I couldn't begin to compete with the other horses.

Sandra knew, but there was nothing she could do about it. That dreadful season was just one long, horrible nightmare, as race after race I tried in vain, knowing that the cough virus had sapped all my strength and what I had left to offer just wasn't enough. My failures depressed me, and if it had not been for Sandra, and not wanting to let her down, I think I would have given up completely.

The height of my ambition that year was to finish the season and rest. Mercifully, at the end of May, Sandra led me out to grass. For two luxurious months, they left me in peace, and I gradually recovered.'

Chapter Five

TROUBLE

'When I was brought in from grass, to begin my training for the new season, I felt in fine form. This year, I was determined to show what I could do.

My trainer now planned to enter me in the novice steeplechases, and a few days before my first 'chase the jockey came up to Oxclose to school me over the fences. I was furious about it – fancy expecting me to practise with a jockey! I'd been really looking forward to getting the hang of those jumps with Sandra, and to see her standing to one side, watching, while someone else put me through my paces was not only distracting, it was asking for trouble. I have to confess that I behaved very badly. I refused the fences and generally made a mess of things.

I listened as the jockey discussed me with my trainer. "We'll just have to run him on Saturday, and hope for the best. I can't see him even finishing the course if he behaves like this."

"Well," replied my trainer, "there's nothing we can do about him now. I don't think that boggy ground is helping, he hates it when it's soft." They walked off, leaving Sandra to take me back to my box.

"Rummie, that was very bad of you." I could tell from her voice that she was more amused than cross. She sprang into the saddle and patted my neck. "How do you think you're going to manage your first 'chase if you behave like that, you silly horse?"

I twitched my ears at her. I was really raring to go at those jumps, and I knew that Sandra could feel the power building up in me. "Right, boy," she shouted. "Let's see what you can *really* do."

We cantered off towards the hurdles and I hardly needed any instructions. We just floated over them, again and again, Sandra enjoying it as much as I was, for I could hear her laughing as we leapt through the air. "Rummie, you're wonderful — run like that on Saturday, and you'll be a steeplechaser."

"You're right, Sandra, he's brilliant." Neither of us had noticed my trainer had come back into the paddock.

For the rest of that week, Sandra continued to school me over the fences. "Right, my Rummie," she said to me, as she prepared me for the race. "Don't forget everything we've learnt. You can do it, I know. Jump like you did for me. Don't you worry about the jockey, just pretend it's me. Now go on in there and show them." '

'What happened?' asked Andy.

'Well, the jockey was surprised, all right. Afterwards, I overheard him telling my trainer that he had half expected me to refuse at the first fence. "Instead, he was good – he jumped like a cat." We finished third and Sandra was so proud about it, it being my very first 'chase, that I decided that the next time I was going to go all out and try for first. I was going to give that next race everything I'd got, and a bit more besides, if necessary.'

Rummie paused, remembering the triumph of that run at Doncaster. Everything had been perfect. The ground was just as he liked it and he had felt so full of power that day . . .

'Did you win?' interrupted Andy.

'Oh yes, I did it, Andy. Not just once, I won a few times. Things were going beautifully and then, halfway through the season, something started to go wrong. My foot didn't feel right. I wasn't lame and there was no way that I could tell Sandra about it. I don't know how to explain it. I just knew that something was going wrong, inside my foot. I decided to ignore the feeling and concentrate on my work. Worrying about my foot wasn't going to help me to win those races. The season wore on and, although I kept going, I was no longer doing as well as I had hoped.

Then came the day of the race at Newbury. As I came down the ramp from the horse-box, a sudden twinge of pain shot up my leg, taking me completely by surprise. My behaviour must have seemed very odd to everyone, for I began to buck and kick and I slipped on the tarmac. I tried to pull myself together and concentrate on the race, but it was no use. Although the pain had gone, it had frightened me badly, and I disappointed everyone with my poor performance.

By the time we got back to Oxclose, I had calmed down. My foot felt fine again, and I began to wonder if I had imagined it. I felt annoyed with myself for going to pieces like that and making such a mess of the race. I must forget about my foot and try to do better, I decided, little knowing what a nightmare lay just three weeks ahead.'

He shuddered at the memory that even time and triumphs had not managed to erase. 'It was the course I had hoped I'd never see again. Slippery, soft going on a racetrack that will always, for me, be clouded by the shame and pain of that first hard race there. Think of Sandra, I told myself. Think of the winning post, nothing else matters. I started the race full of grim determination, trying to ignore the sticky, squelching turf. As we approached the hurdles, the jockey urged me forward and I leapt, dreading that split second later, when my front hoof would hit the treacherous mud with such violence, carrying the full brunt of my weight. As I landed, I felt again that chilling stab of pain. It jarred back up my leg and vibrated along every nerve. The jockey was pressing me onwards. I can't let that happen, I remember thinking. He isn't going to have that power over me. I forgot my pain and ran, managing to finish fourth.'

'What happened when they found you were lame?' asked Andy.

'That's just it, Andy. I wasn't lame – I walked to my box quite normally afterwards. No one knew that anything was wrong. My feet would be fine and then suddenly, with no warning at all, I would get this stab of pain when my hoof was under pressure. It would go as swiftly as it had come, and I grew edgy and nervous about it. I felt that I could no longer trust my own foot.

It was around this time that my old trainer retired, and for a while Mr Stack, the jockey who had ridden me most frequently, came to take charge. In some ways, it made things easier for me, to have the same jockey all the time. Constant changes had always unsettled me, for each jockey has a slightly different method of riding. I've already explained that I raced for myself, because I wanted to do it, but I still needed the jockey to help me round the course. Mr Stack, knowing nothing of the disease that was beginning to gnaw into the bones of my foot, thought that I was a disappointing, mediocre sort of animal and accused me of not trying. It was very unpleasant for me, to have to stand there and listen to those criticisms, for I knew that they were not deserved. Sandra loyally tried to make excuses for me and I longed to be able to tell her about my foot.

One morning, I waited and waited for her in my box, and she did not come. The first lot of horses had already been led out for exercise and I was left behind, wondering why she was not there. I listened out for her, but all remained silent until the stable lads clattered back into the yard.

"You'd better take Red out now," called Mr Stack. "Sandra is going to be off for a while."

I pricked up my ears. Why had she gone away without telling me? I knew that I hadn't done as well as she had hoped, but I couldn't believe that she would give me up.

"How is she?" asked one of the boys.

"Poorly," replied Mr Stack. "It was a nasty fall. Even Sandra couldn't hold that madhead and he fell on the bend. She smashed into the railings and the hospital says her collar bone is crushed. It's going to take a few weeks to mend."

The next weeks were the most miserable that I have ever spent. Life wasn't the same without Sandra and I could hardly bear to face each new day. I didn't even care about my foot any more. It didn't seem to matter, now.

One morning, as I stood moping in my box, our old trainer came into the yard. He walked down the row and stopped in front of me. "This horse looks terrible," he shouted. "He's pining. You might just as well take him out of training altogether, he'll do no good like that. When is Sandra due back?"

"Not for another week or two," replied Mr Stack.

"Well, I'm going to have a word with her. If she can't come back right away, there's no point in carrying on with him."

The next morning, it was just getting light when I saw her coming round the corner of the yard. I whinnied to her.

"Rummie," she cried, running over to me. "Rummie, I'm here." She opened the door and flung her arms around my neck. "Oh, Rummie, I have missed you. Let me look at you."

She stood back and I watched the pleasure vanish from her face. "Oh Rummie, what's happened to you? You look terrible – so thin and rough . . . "

Angrily, she turned to Mr Stack. "What have you done to him? You've neglected him, haven't you? He's been starved . . . "

"Now stop that, Sandra. Of course we haven't neglected him. He refused to eat – he's done that to himself. I told you, if you don't come back to do him, we're taking him out of training."

"Oh, no, you're not," said Sandra. "I'm back. Rummie and I can convalesce together. I'll soon build him up again for you."

She turned to me. "I'll not have you going around looking like that – you'd better pull yourself together, boy – fast."

So I let her boss me around a bit and was very gentle with her, for I knew that her shoulder was not properly better.

Soon afterwards we had a new trainer, Mr Gillam, a friend of Mr Stack's. Mr Stack had decided he preferred being a jockey to being a trainer, but we were to meet again, often.

Mr Gillam was nice and understanding, except that he didn't know about my foot going wrong, either. He was young, and anxious to make a success of Oxclose, which had been a very famous stable under the old trainer.

I felt a lot better now that Sandra was back and she travelled over to Haydock with me. "Do well, Rummie," she begged me. "This is our first race under Mr Gillam – show him what you can do."

I looked at her helplessly. If only I could have told her about my foot. There was a dull, nagging ache in it now, most of the time, and although I tried my hardest, I only came in fourth. I could tell as soon as I got back to the paddock that they were disappointed.

"He's blowing a bit," said Mr Gillam. It was perfectly true, for the pain had grown worse during the race and it was making me pant.

Sandra felt my legs. "There's a bit of heat in this off-fore, Mr Gillam."

Mr Gillam told her to walk me round and he watched carefully. "He's not lame. I don't think that's anything to worry about, Sandra. We'll hose it down and poultice it; there might be a little inflammation in the fetlock joint. I'm more concerned with the way he's blowing – he's still out of condition. Needs a lot more work. I want him really fit for Catterick and it's only ten days away."

For the next week, Sandra took me out on long, strenuous gallops. "Come on," she urged. "Show them all what you can do. Let's show them that you are fit again, I want you to win the next one." '

Andy, who had been listening in stunned silence, could contain himself no longer. 'Why on earth didn't you start limping, Rummie? Then they would have guessed that something was wrong. That's what I would have done – you must be mad.'

'I couldn't do a thing like that, Andy. I couldn't cheat them, Sandra and Mr Gillam. The next race was important for him, having just taken over. It wouldn't have been right, to let them down like that. In any case, I'd grown used to the aching in my foot. It had been there for so long, by then, that I'd almost learnt to live with it. I ignored it and carried on. I was determined to win that race for them – and I did.

It cost me dear, though, for I came back truly lame. For several days afterwards I couldn't bear to put any weight on my foot. I hobbled round like a cripple, but at least, then, they knew that something was wrong. Mr Gillam brought in someone to look at me, and Sandra stayed with me, anxiously listening to the conversation. "I can't find anything obviously wrong," said the gentleman, after a great deal of probing. "I think we had better get this foot X-rayed." '

Chapter Six

FIGHTING BACK

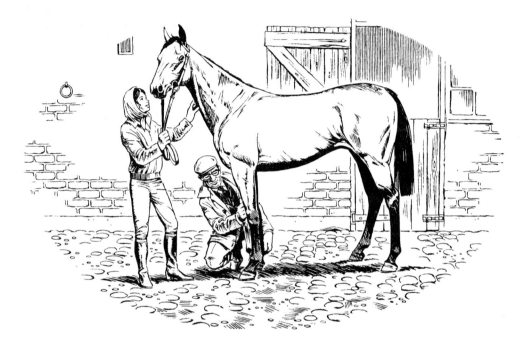

'The next morning, when Sandra was grooming me, Mr Gillam came into the yard. With him was the gentleman who had examined me the previous day.

Sandra stopped brushing. "Stay quiet, Rummie, it's the vet." We stood listening as they drew nearer to my box.

"I'm very sorry about it," the vet was saying. "The outlook isn't good. I'm afraid very few horses get over it. Did you say he actually won that race at Catterick? Incredible, he must have been running in great pain. It's a wonder that he even finished the course. You've got a very courageous animal there."

Sandra glanced across at Mr Gillam. "What is it? What's wrong with him?"

Mr Gillam looked very serious. "Without going into all the details, it's a bone disease, very similar to arthritis in a human. It must have been causing him a great deal of pain for quite some time. You can imagine the sort of impact that diseased foot has had to support every time his whole weight landed on it."

Sandra was aghast. "Poor Rummie – and the way we've made him work." She turned to the vet. "Can you cure it?"

The vet shrugged his shoulders. "We can try, but there are no guarantees of success. The chances, at the most, are fifty-fifty. Physiotherapy will help him, but it's going to be expensive."

Sandra bit her lip.

"Don't worry too much, Sandra," said Mr Gillam. "We'll try everything we can for him."

"So he's not to be ridden any more?" asked Sandra sadly.

"On the contrary," replied the vet. "He needs long, slow exercise each day. Just gentle walking on level ground, nothing strenuous. Keep the whole foot poulticed and get the blacksmith to make him a special hoof pad. We'll start him on the physiotherapy right away, three times a week, and see how he progresses. Only time will tell."

He was just turning to leave when he caught sight of the misery on Sandra's face. "Don't be too downhearted," he told her. "I've a great deal of faith in this ultrasonic therapy. It's something fairly new in animal medicine, but I've seen it work miracles before now." He handed her a course of tablets. "These will lessen the pain. We'll do all we can for him, but the rest is up to you. Remember – long, slow daily exercise – no clever stuff."

I felt tremendously relieved, now that they knew about my foot and I was allowed to take things easily. Each day, throughout the rest of the winter, Sandra and I would set off on our own and wander wherever we pleased. It was like being on holiday, for we were no longer subjected to the routine of the yard. Every morning, we left the stables far behind and ambled off into the surrounding countryside. Sometimes we started out so early that the lanes would still be silver with frost, glinting in the first sunlight, and the air was so sharp that my breath would steam before me. Everywhere smelt so fresh that my spirits lifted and I longed to canter over the misty fields that surrounded us.

Sandra, sensing my mood, held me back firmly. "Not yet, Rummie. Be patient, we mustn't spoil things."

Three times a week the physiotherapist came to give me my ultrasonic treatments. I was nervous the first time I saw the strange machine. Attached to it was a small round disc, which he used to massage all around my foot. After the treatment I could feel an odd, tingling sensation but it was not unpleasant and I soon became used to it. Week by week I improved, and when the vet came to look at me he was pleased with my progress.

"Is he going to be all right?" asked Sandra.

The vet smiled at her. "Let's just say that there is every reason to be optimistic. We'll carry on with the treatments and I think you could gradually start to build him up for work again. Just do a little with him, each day, and don't overdo it, or we'll be right back where we started."

By this time, there was already a faint promise of spring in the air and I felt so much better that I became quite frisky. Sandra caught my mood and, for the first time, we left the lanes and took to the fields. "Easy, Rummie," she cautioned, as I began to build up speed.

A herd of young bullocks looked up in surprise as we cantered towards them. As we drew nearer, they began to panic, jostling together in their clumsy way. One broke loose from the throng and began to rush down the hedgerow and, a moment later, the rest were following in wild stampede.

Sandra reined me to a halt, laughing. "I've always wanted to be a cowgirl, Rummie. Shall we have a bit of fun with them?"

We cantered along in their wake, rounded them up and drove them back over the field. Sandra enjoyed our little game so much that we began to go back to the place whenever we could. Rounding up the bullocks became part of our daily work-out and, not long afterwards, the vet suggested that I might go back into training.

Mr Gillam told Sandra to take things very easily with me. "I want to build him up again, nice and slowly," he explained.

Things went well to begin with. We did a little more work each day and my muscles began to harden. Sandra was pleased with me.

A few days later, Mr Gillam came up to us when we got back to the yard. "We're going to run him at Catterick," he said.

Sandra gasped. "That's only a couple of weeks away. He won't be nearly ready . . ."

Mr Gillam interrupted. "He's got to be ready. You'd better get plenty of work into him, and fast. Your Rummie has got to start earning his keep again. The blacksmith is coming tomorrow. I've asked him to put a protective leather pad between the hoof and his shoes. We'll just have to hope for the best." '

'Did your feet feel all right?' asked Andy.

'More or less, yes. They certainly felt better than they had done for months, but perhaps I shouldn't have been flung back into racing quite so quickly. I certainly hadn't got back into top peak form, but it was good to be back on the track again.

It's funny, I enjoy my breaks immensely, and it's not until I get back to the course that I realise just how much I've missed it. You wouldn't understand, Andy. Please don't mind my saying so, but until you've experienced it, you just can't imagine what it's like. The challenge, the excitement . . .'

'You're right, Rummie. Give me my field any day – saddles, bits and bridles are certainly not my idea of fun.'

'What is?'

'Oh, all sorts of nice simple things. Listening to the birds at dawn, watching the thrush rear her young, over in the far hedge. A good roll in the dust – listening to you, I suppose. Do go on.'

'Where was I up to? Yes, Catterick. Well, it turned out to be a bit of a disaster. I was doing quite well, lying third, when the horse in front of me fell at one of the fences. I tumbled straight over him and for the first time in my life I went down. It really shook me up. I was stiff for days afterwards, and they had to change their plans about entering me for the next race.

Sandra continued to put me through my paces and I began, at last, to feel more powerful. Maybe now, finally, I was on my way to real success. Mr Gillam hoped so, too, and decided to enter me for something big – the Scottish National. I was determined to give that race every ounce that I'd got, for I knew that I would be competing against some really top horses. Even the fact that I had yet another strange jockey wasn't going to deter me. On the day of the race, there was just one tiny cloud that I had not bargained for. My foot began to bother me; not badly, but I was aware of it.

It was certainly something that I could have well done without, especially on an occasion like that. I still ran well, and finished fifth.

The 1973 Grand National: the dreaded Chair – the biggest jump of all. A six-foot-wide ditch is followed by a five-foot, two-inch fence. No wonder so many horses fell – including Glenkiln.

The 1973 Grand National: Red Rum overtakes Crisp, who had led nearly all the way, to pass the winning post three quarters of a head in front.

That is nothing to be ashamed of in a race of that sort, where all the runners are good, but I'd set my sights a lot higher than that. My vet had been watching the race, and he came to us afterwards, in the paddock.

"He's still feeling that foot, I'm afraid," I heard him say. "I would never have noticed it, if I didn't already know about it, but I thought I'd better warn you. Just be on the look-out, in case it gets worse again." '

Chapter Seven

THE PARTING

'I was suddenly overwhelmed with hopelessness. Every single season at Oxclose, I had started out with such ambition and determination, and each year something beyond my control had prevented me from fulfilling my promise. The crying need for grass, followed by that dreadful season of the cough – I'd survived those things, only to be checked by the chilling news of the disease in my foot. I could survive that, too; all I needed was time, to let me get over it properly. I made a real mess of my next race. I just wasn't up to it. None of us knew, then, that it was to be the last that I would ever run from Oxclose.

One afternoon, Sandra and I were just returning from our ride. As we passed the back of the house on our way to the stable yard, the sound of voices drifted through the open window. There was something about them that attracted our attention.

"Quiet, Rummie. Stay still," Sandra whispered. She stiffened and her tension travelled into me.

"It's no use arguing about it — I've made up my mind."

"You're making a big mistake, if you'll pardon my saying so." That was Mr Gillam speaking.

"There's no guarantee that he'll remain sound – it's good money after bad. He's not much good anyway. The jockey thinks he's inconsistent. I'm not prepared to risk another season with him."

"But he's just coming into himself," protested Mr Gillam. "Next season, you'll see – I'm sure he'll do well. If you sell him now, someone else will get all the benefit of what we've worked for – and it would break Sandra's heart."

"I didn't buy him for Sandra," came the reply. "I've made up my mind, so that's the end of it."

Slowly, Sandra led me back to my box and began to prepare my feed, but I could tell from her manner that her thoughts were elsewhere. What we had overheard had set me wondering, too, but nothing was said until a few days later, when Mr Gillam came over to my box.

Sandra just carried on brushing me down, in silence, but the air hummed with tension and I suddenly felt very uneasy. Finally, Mr Gillam spoke. "Sandra, I've got some bad news for you, I'm afraid."

Sandra brushed me even harder and still did not look at him. "I know."

Mr Gillam looked very uncomfortable. "You know? About Rummie?"

"Yes," said Sandra, still brushing away at my flank. "Bad news travels fast."

Mr Gillam cleared his throat. "I've been trying to pluck up the courage to tell you – I didn't know how you'd take it."

Sandra suddenly flung down the brush, startling Mr Gillam and making me jump. "Take it?" she exclaimed. "How do you expect me to take it? What does it matter how I take it? I'm only the one who cares for him – looks after him, gets up off my sickbed to stop him fretting away. I've devoted four years to this horse, and he's had nothing but setbacks. I've helped him to struggle back again and again. Rummie and I have overcome all the problems together. Can't you see? He's just on the brink of getting somewhere at last."

The King of Aintree.

Mr Gillam nodded. "I know, Sandra. I've tried to argue, but it's all settled. He's going to the Doncaster Sales."

Sandra picked up the brush again and began polishing my coat. After a few minutes, she spoke. "Eleven years, I've been here, Mr Gillam. I've done plenty of good horses in that time, and grown very fond of some of them. And I've seen them go – that's part of the job. But Rummie's different. I just can't believe that we've been through so much together for it to end like this. He'll go, and I'll never know what happens to him."

As I stood there listening, I suddenly felt completely helpless. For the first time, I realised how little we horses are masters of our own fate.

"He may not go . . . "

Sandra swung round and I could see the flicker of hope on her face.

"I might buy him myself," said Mr Gillam. "I'm going to try to raise the money, with some friends. It depends how high the bidding goes. Don't take him out in the morning. The vet's coming to check him over, then he can be issued with a certificate of soundness."

I stood quietly in the yard with Sandra, while the vet examined me. Mr Gillam came over. "Are his feet all right?"

The vet nodded. "Yes, I can pronounce him completely sound."

Mr Gillam smiled. "That's a relief. I'm going to try and buy him myself."

The vet looked at him sharply. "I wouldn't go spending too much money on him, if I were you. His feet are fine again now, but they might not stay right for ever. The chances of the disease starting up again are about fifty-fifty."

After he had left, Mr Gillam came over to Sandra. "You heard what the vet said, Sandra. Don't pin your hopes on it – I can't really afford him and his feet do worry me a bit. If the bidding gets high, I'll have to drop out." He turned to go.

"Mr Gillam," called Sandra. "He's qualified, you know – he could be a National horse."

Mr Gillam looked at her anxious face. "I know, Sandra – but just because I'm involved with racehorses, that doesn't make me a gambling man."

A few day after this conversation had taken place, Mr Gillam was again waiting for us when we got back from exercise. "I've got a bit more bad news for you, I'm afraid. They're not going to let you take him to the sale."

Sandra, who had been very irritable all week, suddenly flew into a rage. "Why ever not?" she snapped. "After the way I've looked after Rummie . . . "

"That's just it," said Mr Gillam. "They're afraid you'll get upset and make a scene. Just think about it a little. Don't you think it would be better for you to say goodbye to him here?"

After the 1973 Grand National: police horses flank the winner, ridden by Brian Fletcher and led by Billy.

Sandra put me into my box and leant on the door. It was the first time that either of us had actually thought about the moment when we would have to part. After a long time, she turned to Mr Gillam. "Right, Mr Gillam. That's it, then, I'm leaving. I'm finished with racehorses for good. I'll go at the end of the week."

"Don't be hasty, Sandra. This is your whole way of life. Whatever would you do with yourself?"

Sandra picked moodily at the edge of my stable door with her finger-nail. "There is someone . . . " She looked up and blushed. "Someone who has been waiting for me for a long time. I never would before, because of Rummie. Now, there's nothing really to keep me here. I'm going to get married."

She picked up my saddle and strode off to the tackroom. Mr Gillam patted me on the neck and followed her.

On Friday evening, when everyone else had left the yard and the horses were all bedded down for the night, she came to my box. As we stood there, in the straw, she pressed her head hard into my neck and I could feel her tears. I nuzzled her shoulder, trying to comfort her.

"Don't pine for me, Rummie," she whispered. "Keep on trying. I know you can do it. You don't need me."

That was the worst part of all, not being able to talk back to her. I nuzzled her again, trying to show that I did need her. She pushed my head away. "Stop it, Rummie. I can't bear it."

I pulled myself up, tall and straight, hoping that I looked brave.

The sound of footsteps echoed across the yard. "Sandra," called a voice. "Sandra, are you there? I've been waiting for you."

Sandra blew her nose and leant out of my box. A young man stood outside. "I thought you'd be here," he said gently. "Come on, it's time to go."

He looked up at me. "So this is my rival, is it? This is the great Rummie."

"Oh, Bryan, I'm so worried about him. If he starts to pine, he'll go right down again. The worst bit is not being able to explain to him."

"Sandra," said the young man. "I don't know much about horses, but I do think that animals understand a lot more than we think. You've done as much as you possibly could for him. He must be grateful for that. You've got your own life to lead, now. There's no use in spoiling your future by worrying about him. Miss him, yes, but it's very wrong for any of us to become so dependent on something that life becomes empty without it."

He turned to me. "And that goes for you, too, Rummie. I'm going to look after Sandra, and you must look after yourself. You don't want the poor girl fretting about you, do you?"

"Go and wait in the car, Bryan," said Sandra. "I won't be a moment."

When we were alone together, she put her arms around my neck and drew my head down to hers. We stared at each other and she smiled at me. "Right Rummie – this is it, then. Goodbye." She swallowed hard. "I hope and pray that you fall into good hands."

A second later she was gone, hurrying across the yard. I felt a great whinny rising up into my throat, but I held it there until the sound of the car had faded. I didn't want her to go away thinking that I was less than brave.

I was impatient to leave Oxclose after that. There was too much that reminded me of Sandra. She had already started her new life, and I was anxious to do the same.'

Chapter Eight

DONCASTER SALE

'I travelled over to Doncaster with Mr Gillam and one of the stable lads. Mr Gillam was still hopeful.

"No one's bothered to come over to look at him," I heard him say. "I don't think anyone's that interested, and he's got a high reserve on him now. I think there's a good chance we might be bringing him back home with us."

It no longer mattered to me whether I came back or not. I had left Oxclose without a backward glance and in many ways I was looking forward to going on to somewhere new.

I have already told you what it is like to be paraded round an auction ring and how the vast circle of faces blurs before your eyes. You know that somewhere in that sea of people is a stranger who is trying to buy you, who will take you away with him when it is all over. The feeling is exactly the same whatever the place, and it makes no difference whether you are going to be sold for hundreds or thousands of pounds. Money is meaningless to a horse.

The bids came in swiftly and the price rapidly climbed to the reserve figure set by my owner and Mr Gillam. After that, there were only two men bidding, and one of them was Mr Gillam.

I circled the ring yet again. Mr Gillam made his last bid – he had reached his limit. There was a moment of silence. His opponent called again and both he and the auctioneer thought that I was sold.

Suddenly, a tall man with unruly ginger hair stepped forward. I had not noticed him before. Very clearly, for all to see, he held up the five fingers of his right hand and then added the thumb of his left. Someone gasped.

"Six thousand," called the auctioneer.

All around me, the crowd rustled and the tension was replaced by astonishment. The gavel banged down. As it did so, I looked across the ring at the man. "McCain," he said.

"Sold to Mr McCain," said the auctioneer.

Mr McCain's strained face melted into a delighted smile and I passed quite close to him as I was led back to my box.

Mr Gillam was already there, waiting for me, and he looked so miserable that I felt sorry for him. After a while, Mr McCain appeared.

"You've bought him, have you?" asked Mr Gillam. "What are you going to do with him?"

I pricked up my ears.

"Win a few races, I hope," said Mr McCain. "I'm hoping he might turn out to be a Grand National horse."

The Grand National is about as hard and tough a challenge as you can get – right at the top of the racing tree, you might say. Yet this man was talking about me and the Grand National – me, who began life as a humble sprinter! I had done some steeplechasing, as you know, but all those setbacks had badly bruised my enthusiasm for it. Now, as I listened to the conversation, I realised that my ambition was still there, after all. I warmed to Mr McCain.

"I've always wanted to train a National horse." He spoke wistfully, as if he'd had a lot of setbacks, too.

"Well, it's not beyond the realms of fancy," replied Mr Gillam. "I think he might do it. He's got a lot of potential in there, if you know how to tap it." He looked sad again. "I'm sorry to lose him. Well, he's yours, now. I think you ought to know about his feet – they won't stand up to being bashed on hard ground – keep an eye on them."

Mr Gillam told him where I was up to in my training, again urged him to take care with my feet and then he turned to me. He patted me heavily on the neck and quickly walked away into the crowd.

After he had disappeared I felt suddenly alone in a world full of strangers and panic began to rise up in me. Mr McCain must have realised how I felt, for he came back to me and ran his hand soothingly along my neck. "Well, Red Rum – it's you and me, now. I've really plunged in at the deep end this time. Let's just hope that you and I are going places together."

He looked at me with such pride that my confidence began to return. It was very plain that my acquisition meant a great deal to him and I was glad that he had bought me. I felt certain, now, that he would not be taking me back to some large stables, where I would be just one of a string of promising horses. This man seemed to be offering me something very special – the chance to fulfil his long-standing ambition. Quietly, I followed him to the horse-box, hoping that I had found someone who would help me to fulfil mine. As long as my foot remained sound, of course . . . I pushed the thought aside.

Westwards, over the Pennines, we travelled throughout that hot afternoon, and beyond the tiny window of my box I watched the grey ribbon of road that lay behind us. We travelled for a long time and I munched at my hay-net, content enough, for those few hours, to be suspended between my past and my future.

Mr McCain sat up in front and I listened carefully as he talked to the driver. I was curious to learn more, for I had no clue yet as to my destination.

"I'll call Mr Le Mare, as soon as we've settled him in – he'll be waiting to hear. I'd just love to see his face when I tell him I've bought him a National horse at long last."

"You're very confident," replied the driver. "You haven't even tried him out yet."

Mr McCain looked at his companion in surprise, then he burst out laughing. "No, I haven't, have I? I must sound crackers, sitting here talking like this, but I know, that's all. Don't ask me how or why, Jackie. I just know."

He glanced round at me, as if to make sure that I was still there. "This is the horse – the one good horse that Mr Le Mare and I have been waiting for," he said proudly. "I'm sure of it. All my life, I've been waiting for him."

Listening to such confidence and assurance made me feel like a giant. The last four disappointing years were forgotten, and I could hardly wait to get back into training. Mr McCain was the right man for me, wherever he was taking me to. He was going to get the very best that I had to offer. This was my greatest stroke of luck yet, to have fallen into the hands of a man who, although it was in a different sort of way, cared about me right from the heart, like Sandra. He made me feel very special, just as she had.

It was early evening, but, being August, still light, when we finally stopped. I waited restlessly, listening as they fumbled outside, and I heard the ramp go down. A moment later, the doors were opened and Mr McCain took hold of my halter. "Come on, Red Rum – we're home."

I stopped at the top of the ramp and looked about me, thinking that there must be some mistake. I could see neither yard nor field and there was no sign of any stable or loose-box. We were parked in a street of shops and houses and straight in front of me was a forecourt of parked cars. Suddenly, there came a strange, unfamiliar rumbling which quickly grew louder. It frightened me so badly that I struggled to get back into the horse-box.

Mr McCain kept a tight hold on me and called to the driver. "That's one thing he's never been used to, Jackie."

The driver laughed. "He soon will be. By next week he won't even notice it."

"Come on, Red – it's only a train," said Mr McCain. "Nothing to get alarmed about. It's not going to hurt you."

I followed him down the ramp and looked anxiously to my right. The awful noise had begun to fade away and I watched in amazement as a pair of gates slowly swung open, as if by magic.

"You'll soon get used to the level crossing, lad. It's a way of life on Aughton Road."

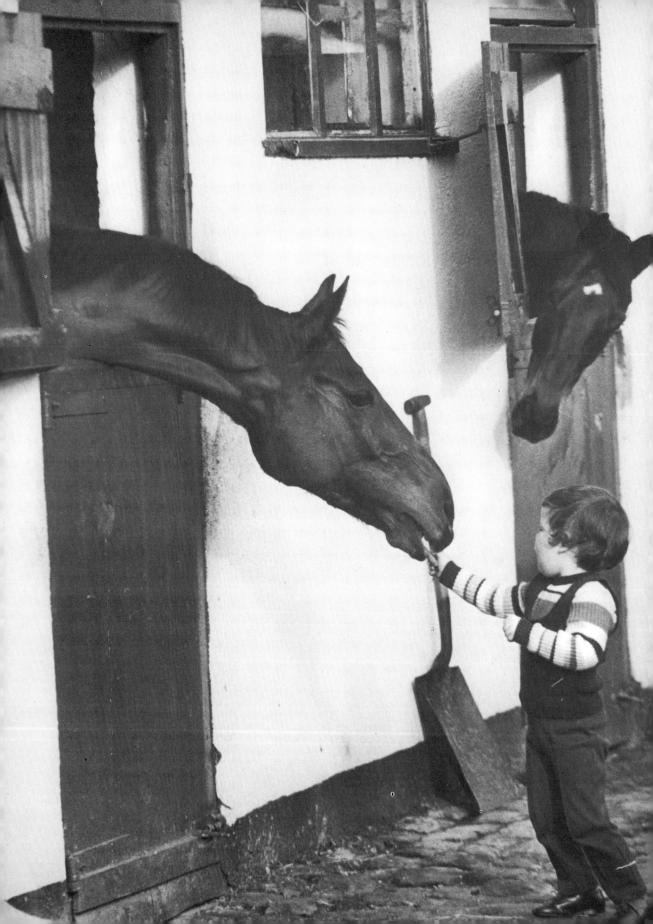

I looked up, beyond the rooftops. The sky was strange here, unusually pale – light and empty. I sniffed the air. Even the smell was
different, yet at the same time, vaguely familiar.

I had no further time to ponder, however, for Mr McCain grasped my
halter firmly and led me between the rows of parked cars. We turned
into a narrow alleyway between two buildings and, at the top, he
opened a tall white gate.

I was surprised to find myself in a small cobbled yard. Two rows of
boxes lined the sides. The air of tranquillity contrasted sharply with
the busy road that masked its presence. It was a pleasant and peaceful
place. Mr McCain led me over to the first box and left me to recover
from the long day.

I looked curiously at my new surroundings. One box is much the
same as another, but my new home was large and airy, and I felt
comfortable there, despite the strangeness. I leant over the door to take
a closer look at the yard. From the opposite row, two other horses stared
back at me. Above, I could see a narrow strip of that strange, pale sky,
now beginning to grow deeper as the evening advanced.

I sniffed again, trying to jog the chord of memory that that tangy air
evoked. What was it, that smell? I had experienced it before, but not
recently. The memory came from long ago. Something I could taste –
salty. That was it, I could taste salt. It tasted like the docks at Dublin,
when they loaded me on to the boat. I breathed it in deeply and my
blood quickened with excitement. It was the sea — that was it! Wherever Mr McCain had brought me, we were close to the sea.'

Red Rum quickly became part of the McCain family and soon made
friends with the children.

Chapter Nine

NEW FRIENDS

'Early the next morning, Mr McCain came to my box with his wife and their two children. The children were excited. As I ate my feed, they hovered in the doorway, watching.

"Bring him out into the yard, Daddy. We want to see him properly."

"Let him finish his breakfast," said Mr McCain. "And you must go and get yours, too. We'll bring him out afterwards."

"I don't want any breakfast," said the girl.

"Neither do I," echoed her small brother. "I'm not hungry – I want to see Red Rum."

Mr McCain leaned out of my box. "No breakfast – no Red Rum."

"Oh, please, Daddy."

Mrs McCain was already on her way back to the house and I watched as she climbed the steps which led to her kitchen. The stable yard was straight off the house and if I leaned out far enough I could see her at the sink, doing the dishes.

"Go on, kids," whispered Mr McCain. "Hurry up, or you'll have your mother after us. If you're quick you'll be back in time to watch me walking him round the yard."

The children were soon back, and Mr McCain, who seemed almost as excited as they were, led me out. By this time, two or three other people had appeared, including Billy, who was to be my new stable lad.

As Mr McCain paraded me up and down, they all leant against the wall. "Well," he said. "What do you think?"

At first no one spoke and then Billy said, "He's magnificent. There's nothing else in the yard to compare with that."

"Now, Billy, be careful what you say. Don't let Glenkiln hear you – he'll be getting upset."

"I wouldn't want to upset Glen," said Billy. "He's a grand horse, but you've got to admit – well, just look at this one – he's a real smasher, Mr McCain."

"So he should be – he cost about six times more than anything else we've ever had in this yard. Mr Le Mare is coming round to see him later, so you get on now and groom him till he shines."

I must admit that I enjoyed all the praise and admiration. Never had I received such glowing compliments and, although I remained in the yard throughout that first day, I was the centre of attention and had no time to grow restless.

By the end of the morning I was beginning to feel quite a celebrity, as Mr McCain proudly showed me off to the people who had come to see me.

Mr Le Mare, my new owner, finally appeared. He was a smartly dressed old gentleman and his dark suit and bowler hat seemed strangely out of place in the yard. For a long time, he just stood looking at me, then he turned to Mr McCain.

"Well, Ginger – this time I think we might have done it. We've got the horse, now the rest is up to you. It's the last ambition I've got and I've been dreaming about it for sixty-seven years. If I can win that Grand National – just once . . . "

He turned to me. "Do that for me, Red Rum, and I'll die a happy old man."

As I watched him leave, I was proud to think that he should consider me worthy to fulfil the dream of a lifetime.

Each afternoon, until four o'clock, is rest time. The bustling activity of the morning suddenly subsides and the stable lads, who have been working since half past six, go off to their quarters for a couple of hours' break.

The yard falls silent and still, the horses doze and the only movement is the fluttering of some cheeky sparrows. As soon as everyone leaves, they come down from the roof tops and the elm tree, to squabble amongst themselves on the cobbles. Occasionally, one will fly right into my box, hopeful that I might have left a few crumbs of oats or bran, but he is usually disappointed.

Red Rum and Billy lead the McCain horses through the streets of Southport

That first afternoon was warm and I stood drowsing, with my head hanging out over the stable door. I was almost asleep when a movement from the next box caught my attention. I looked round.

"Settling in all right? That was quite a reception you got this morning. Even I didn't get all that fuss when I arrived." My neighbour began to rub his chin against the edge of his door.

"Hello, I'm Red Rum," I said, thinking that I had better introduce myself.

"You don't need to tell me that," replied my neighbour. He stopped rubbing his chin and peered round the door at me. "We've had nothing but talk of Red Rum all week. We didn't think Mr McCain would come back from Doncaster without you. He'd really set his heart on you, you know."

I could think of nothing to say and we stood in silence for a few minutes. Then my neighbour continued, "I'm Glenkiln – Glen to my friends. You wouldn't be here, you know, if it wasn't for me."

Greatly surprised, I peered round my door. "That's an odd thing to say – how can you think that, Glen?"

"Well," he explained, "as you must have already gathered, all they want in the whole world – Mr Le Mare and Mr McCain – is to run a horse in the Grand National. It's all they ever talk about, and that was why they bought me. I was already qualified to enter, and getting along very nicely with the training.

"Unfortunately, Mr McCain made a mistake when he filled in the entry forms. The entry was rejected and I was not allowed to run. They were bitterly disappointed, and so was I. That's how they came to buy you.

"They've got high hopes as far as you're concerned and I'm sure that Mr McCain won't make the same mistake twice. It's up to you now, Red Rum. You're the one in the limelight. I hope you feel up to the challenge."

"Oh, I do, Glen, I do. I just hope that you don't resent my being here. I had no idea that I had been brought in to take your place."

Glen snorted. "When you know me better, you will realise that I'm not that small minded. I wish you all the luck in the world. We'll all enjoy whatever glories you bring back from the track. This is a happy little yard, as you'll see for yourself. They've got a way of making you

64   *On Southport Sands.*

feel very special. It works wonders for one's self-confidence."

"Yes, I already sensed that," I replied. "I won't let them down, Glen. I want to do well and I'm delighted to have the chance."

"Don't get the wrong impression about me, by the way," Glen said sternly. "I'm not finished, you know – not by a long chalk. I intend to get myself requalified during this coming season. I'm not going to let a clerical error keep me away from Aintree."

"Will we be going out together?" I asked.

"Oh, yes. I expect we'll be running together tomorrow. They'll be anxious to see what you can do. As a matter of fact, I'm quite looking forward to it myself. You look like the sort I can have a good work-out with. There's nothing like a bit of friendly rivalry to get the old hooves pounding."

"By the way, Glen, where do we go for exercise? I've seen no sign of any fields or open spaces – nothing at all that looks like a gallop."

"Wait till the morning," said Glen mysteriously. "You'll see."

Just then, the lads returned to the yard and I had no chance to question Glen further.

The next morning, after a long and thorough grooming session, which I never enjoy, Billy tacked me up and led me out into the yard. Glen was already there, with his lad in the saddle, so I made a bit of a show, dancing around the cobbles. Billy, one foot in the stirrup, danced with me.

I played about for a few moments before I let Billy mount. It would never do for Glen to think that I was lacking in spirit. He watched me with some amusement and whispered, as we set out through the white gates, "Save it for later, Rummie. Take it easy while we're on the roads, they're busy."

I followed him up the narrow passageway and he led the way between the rows of parked cars. The sound of the traffic was quite unnerving, and I was glad that he was with us. The busy life of a town road was not something that I had ever been used to. I was relieved when we had gone over the level crossing, with its strange gates that opened and closed all by themselves.

Eventually, we turned off into quieter places. Now there were trees and gardens and the houses were much larger, but I paid them scant attention. Something else was distracting me. With each minute that passed, the smell of the sea was growing steadily stronger and it took a tremendous effort to remain at a sedate walking pace.

Suddenly the road just petered out and before us lay a jumble of grassy hillocks and ridges, so steep that it was impossible to see what lay beyond. I stopped, ears pricked. Faintly, travelling along on the wind that gusted over the top of the ridge, came a strange clamour of shrieking and screaming.

I began to quiver with alarm, and then I felt Billy patting my neck. "Easy, lad. That's something else you'll get used to. Another week and the din of the gulls will be music to your ears!"

Firmly, he squeezed me on and I continued to follow Glenkiln along the steep, narrow paths that twisted upwards. It was hard work. My hooves slid down again at every step and I wondered about the strange substance up which we clambered: it was so fine and dry that it trickled down like water when my hooves disturbed it.

The grass, too, was peculiar. Coarse and tufty, it appeared to be completely inedible. Low bushes straggled the sides of our path and they grew sideways, as though they had long ago given up the struggle of remaining upright against the wind.

Finally, our climb ended and we stood on level ground. At last I was able to look around. Ahead of us lay the sea, so endless that it seemed to stretch right into the sky itself. Immediately below spread miles and miles of wide flat beach, the colour of ripe corn.

As I watched, a land-rover began to move slowly along, dragging something in its wake which left a wide, harrowed ribbon in the flat sand. As my eyes travelled again over that great emptiness, a strange, new feeling bubbled up within me. The wind lifted my mane, the gulls screamed and my nostrils flared as I breathed in that glorious smell of the sea. We have climbed up the dunes many times since that first morning, and the overwhelming joy when I get that first glimpse of the unending beach below is always the same.

A moment later, I was following Glenkiln down the steep path that leads to the beach. By now, I was excited and over-eager as I stumbled down the track. When I finally reached the beach, I was dismayed to find that the old dull, nagging sensation had returned to my foot.

We stood waiting as the land-rover came slowly towards us. Mr McCain jumped out. "How was he, Billy?"

Billy held my rein firmly. "All right – a bit eager, I think. He got rather excited when we reached the top of the dunes."

"I've harrowed a two-mile strip. Just canter him, to begin with. We'll see how he warms up."

As we set off, my foot felt terrible, and I knew that it showed. Mr McCain drove up alongside us. "Pull him up, Billy," he shouted. "He's lame. I've bought a lame horse."

He got out of the land-rover and we all stood there on the sands. Poor Mr McCain looked really dismayed. He stared at me disbelievingly, and I saw his throat move as he swallowed hard, trying to choke back the disappointment.

"What do you want me to do with him?" asked Billy.

Mr McCain looked about him helplessly. His eyes travelled along the harrowed strip, after the retreating figure of Glenkiln. Finally he turned back to me and I was filled with that old, depressing sense of hopelessness.

Suddenly, he gestured towards the sea. "There, Billy. Take him over there – walk him in the sea. Keep him out of the way, while we exercise Glen." He stood watching miserably as I limped off towards the shoreline.'

Riding the sand-dunes with Billy.

Chapter Ten

THE SEA HORSE

'As we drew nearer to the sea the sand became wet and heavy, and my weight drew the salt water to the surface. I picked my way carefully through the little coils of sand that the sandworms had left. It was much farther than I had thought.

We had almost reached the water's edge when the sea suddenly came forward to meet me. I stood still as the wave scurried towards us and splashed over my front feet. A moment later the wave gushed back into the tide. Billy squeezed me forward and I walked right into the sea. The shock of cold water was strangely soothing and soon the waves were lapping against my chest.

"That's far enough, Red," said Billy. "We're not going swimming, you know. I haven't got my trunks on!"

He turned me to the right and we walked along. It was an odd sensation, pushing that shifting weight of water before me at every step. After a few minutes, we came back into shallows and now the sound of my splashing was added to the breaking of the waves. My feet and legs began to tingle and the sensation reminded me of my ultrasonic treatments.

After a while, Mr McCain called us. "Better bring him out now, Billy."

As we walked back up the beach, I was surprised and delighted to find that my feet were now perfect. Mr McCain stared at me. "He's sound," he said disbelievingly. "He's walking sound."

"And he's raring to go," added Billy. "I can really feel him building up. Shall I run him?"

Mr McCain nodded. "Aye, take him up the strip, but see that you take it easy with him."

Although he didn't know it, he was asking the impossible of poor Billy. I was so overjoyed to find the pain in my foot had disappeared, as if by magic, that, seeing the long, harrowed strip lying ahead of me, stretching off into the distance, I just set off and ran.

With the wind whistling between my ears, and the gulls screaming, I went faster and faster. As my hooves thundered over the sand, I quite forgot about Billy. This was utterly different from anything I had ever known. The harrowed surface was soft and yielding as my feet landed upon it, and yet beneath it remained reassuringly firm and solid. It contained no secret pitfalls, as grass often does, nor did it jar on my hooves, like running on hard ground. This was firm sand, and I knew that I could trust it. The farther I ran, the more powerful I seemed to grow, and after a few minutes I felt as though I was flying.

At the end of the strip we turned, and I raced back down the beach to Mr McCain. I stood quietly while Billy dismounted. He was breathless.

Mr McCain shook his head. "I'm speechless, Billy. I set off after you in the land-rover and I couldn't catch you. I told you to take it easy with him."

"It wasn't me," Billy protested, gasping. "Next time, you tell *him* to take it easy with me. I couldn't hold him. I've never known anything like it, Mr McCain. I was just a passenger up there, clinging on for dear life."

Billy ran his hand along my neck. "Just look at that, he isn't even sweating. We've just galloped four miles, at breakneck speed, and he stands there cool as a cucumber. This horse is tremendous, it's like – " he paused, searching for a suitable comparison " – like driving a Jaguar when you've only ever been in old bangers before. Mr McCain, this horse has got gears that you've never even dreamed about."

Mr McCain's eye twinkled. "I'll see you back at the yard. See you wash him down well. He's still sticky with sea-water."

We clambered back over the sand-dunes and on to the quiet roads, which gradually became busier as we neared the yard. At the level crossing, we had to wait while a train hurtled by and I tried to side-step in panic. Billy held me firmly. When we entered the yard, Glen was already in his box, feeding. He glanced over the door questioningly, and I knew that he must be wondering why I'd been so long.

As soon as everyone had gone, he called, "What happened at the beach? I thought we were going to have a work-out together?"

I explained about my foot, and how it had suddenly gone bad again. Glen listened sympathetically and when I had finished he said, "You've come to the right place then, Rummie. Your feet will be like new again."

"It's the sea, isn't it?" I said.

Glen nodded. "I've heard some amazing tales about what the sea can do. Mr McCain knows; he's got great faith in the sea. When he was a child, they still used old, broken-down horses to pull the shrimping carts through the tide. I've heard him say that, after a couple of seasons working along the shore, their legs would be perfect again. They always take me into the water to cool off after exercise, and it really tones you up. I'm sure that I don't need to tell you, after your experiences, but if your legs feel good, so does the rest.'"

'Was Glen right?' asked Andy.

Rummie nodded. 'Absolutely – from that day to this, I've never had a moment's trouble with my feet. The sea provided me with a completely natural cure. There it was, just down the road, always waiting for me when I went for exercise. I often wonder what would have become of me if I hadn't ended up by the sea. Nothing could

The 1974 Grand National: jumping Becher's Brook for the second time. Red Rum is in the lead and L'Escargot, who finished second, is the horse on the right.

replace the beach for me: galloping along those wide open spaces, where the going never varies, whatever the weather. After a few weeks, I was far advanced in my training; horses that have to work on the more conventional sort of gallops are always at the mercy of the weather.'

'Then why don't they train all racehorses on the sand?' asked Andy.

'Most trainers don't approve,' Rummie explained. 'They say that the sand is hard and unyielding, bad for the feet.

It was quite by chance that Mr McCain stumbled on the secret of running horses on sand. Glen told me how he once exercised a horse on the beach and it cut a tendon on a piece of broken glass that had been left lying around. Ever since that happened, Mr McCain has always harrowed a strip to ensure that it is clear of any dangerous rubbish.

The harrowing also breaks up the surface, so that the hoof comes down, not on to hard sand, but into a soft cushioning layer that absorbs the strain of the impact. Whatever they say, it suits me; and afterwards I walk about in the waves to cool off. Since I came to Southport, I've never looked back.

Billy took me down to the beach most days, and Glen and I,

together with the other horses from the yard, exercised on the harrowed strip.

One morning, I overheard Jackie talking to Billy. "You're breaking Glen's heart. He just can't keep up with that Red Rum of yours."

"Well, you surely don't expect me to hold Red back, do you? It will keep Glen up to the mark anyway – he's had front place all to himself for long enough."

For the past few days, Glen had been very quiet and, that afternoon, I decided to talk to him.

"Is everything all right, Glen?"

Glen peered round his door. "Yes, Rummie, I'm fine. Don't you worry yourself about me." He stared moodily across the yard.

"Have I upset you?" I continued.

He looked at me rather sadly. "It isn't your fault, Rummie. It's just – well, seeing you coming along so – you go down that strip like a cannonball now. I've been matched against a lot of fast horses in my time, and I wouldn't want it any other way, but you're incredible. You've just made me realise my own limitations, I suppose. You're going to give somebody a tough time in the Grand National – and good luck to you."

I could think of nothing to say. We stared out into the yard in silence.

Eventually, Glen spoke again. "You're going up to Carlisle next week. I heard them talking this morning – Mr McCain has entered you for the three-mile handicap."

This news pleased me. It seemed a long time since I had been on a racetrack and I was anxious to see whether I could keep up the same sort of speed there that I was now able to achieve along the sands.

"Did they say who was to be my jockey?" I asked Glen, who somehow manages to know everything that goes on.

"No one I know," he answered. "Someone called Tommy – Tommy Stack, I think it was. Do you know him?"

I nodded. "He used to ride me a lot when I was at Oxclose. He even acted as my trainer for a while. He doesn't think much of me, I'm afraid. I was going through a pretty rough patch when he knew me."

"He's in for a bit of a surprise then," said Glen. "That should make you twice as keen to show your paces."

The 1974 Grand National: Red Rum and Brian Fletcher pass the winning post well clear of the rest.

When we arrived at the Carlisle track, it soon became obvious that, of the four runners, I was the scorned outsider. A horse called Gyleburn was easily the favourite, and both the other runners had already been out and done well at the beginning of this new season.

Mr McCain was little-known, and generally regarded as a small-town trainer who was unlikely to present anything of real consequence. Knowing this, the whole outing was something of an adventure for both of us – our joint debut. I think I was the more confident.

Shortly before the race was due to start, Mr Stack came up to us in the paddock. He stood chatting to Mr McCain.

"I think Red Rum's going to do well, Tommy."

Mr Stack looked at him sharply. "Now don't go expecting too much of this horse, Ginger. We won't beat Gyleburn, you know. We haven't a chance of that. This one always needs a couple of runs before he's anywhere near ready. I know him, this is his first run of the season and he won't have warmed up yet."

"I think you may be surprised," said Mr McCain, coolly, and I could have sworn that he winked at me.

By the time we had cleared the third fence, it was just me and Gyleburn, duelling neck and neck around the track. After two and a half miles, I really began to warm up. I saved a final burst for the moment that the winning line came into view, then I drew powerfully ahead to win by three quarters of a length. Everyone at the track, apart from Mr McCain and Billy, was amazed. Mr Stack rode me into the winner's enclosure, got off and stood back.

He looked up at me and shook his head. "Well, Ginger – I don't know what you've done to him, but what a difference! This is not the horse I used to know. How long have you had him?"

"Six weeks," said Mr McCain. "It's just over six weeks since he arrived."

"Well, whatever it is, he's a credit to you," said Mr Stack. "Quite astonishing. It will be interesting to see how he gets on this season."

Mr McCain grinned. " You'll see, Tommy. We haven't even started yet . . .""

Chapter Eleven

THE TIDE TURNS

'Our Carlisle victory was, indeed, only the beginning. Mr Stack had been right about me – I was different, because I felt different.

For most of my racing life, I had run only for myself. Whatever triumphs I had gained had been lonely ones, shared only with Sandra.

Now that I was at Southport, I had become the main cornerstone of a dedicated trio. My owner, my trainer and I were all chasing the same thing, and it was something far more important than money. What we were after was glory, and it was now waiting, invisible but powerful, at the end of every track.

My long, lonely years of setback and failure only served to make the joys of victory seem all the sweeter. The next weeks were the happiest and most rewarding that I had ever known.

Only one thing marred my pleasure – I felt sad about Glenkiln. He appeared not to mind, and was always pleased for me when I returned to the yard after another successful race, but his fine, sporting attitude made me feel bad. Success was something I could not share with him.

"Rummie, do stop feeling guilty about me," he ordered, when I finally confided my feelings. "You're underrating me – just you wait. I'm going to Liverpool next week, and I intend to win. I told you before, I'm not finished yet."

When they brought him back to his box after the race, there was a cocky jauntiness about him that had been sadly lacking in the previous few weeks.

"Well, Glen?" I asked, as soon as they had settled him down. "What happened?"

He looked at me with shining eyes. "Twelve lengths," he said.

"Pardon?"

"Twelve whole lengths," he repeated, as if he couldn't quite believe it. "I left the opposition standing, Rummie. Licked the lot of them by twelve lengths." He sighed happily. "And that's not all – this win has requalified me for the Grand National. I'll be running with you, Rummie. We'll both be there." There cannot have been a happier pair of horses anywhere, that night, than Glen and I.

Our lads were grooming us the next morning when Mr McCain appeared from the house. He was waving a handful of newspapers and grinning from ear to ear. "Look, lads – just look at these headlines."

Billy stopped brushing me and took the papers from him. He began to read aloud: "SEASIDE SCENE'S SUCCESS SECRET." "TIDE TURNS FOR GINGER MCCAIN." "THE GREMLINS RELENT – GLENKILN WINS." "MCCAIN SWEARS BY SEASIDE TRAINING."

"There's a pile of telegrams, too," said Mr McCain, looking proudly at Glen and me. "Who would have believed it? Two National horses, after all these years. We're on our way at last, lads. Red Rum and Glenkiln have put the McCain stables on the map."

At Haydock, in the Southport Handicap 'Chase, I totted up my fourth consecutive win. This was an especially proud moment for the yard, because it was the first time that the race had been won by a Southport owner. In addition to the prize money, we were ceremoniously presented with a special paddock sheet by the Mayoress. Word was beginning to spread and now it seemed that the whole town was behind Mr McCain in his hopes for the Grand National.

"RED RUM AND THE SEA ARE UNBEATABLE," shouted Billy.

"Don't be so arrogant," said Jackie.

"I'm not," said Billy. "I'm just reading the *Daily Mail*."

We were down on the beach again, and Glen and I had just galloped neck and neck down the strip.

"I think we'd better rest him for a bit," said Mr McCain. "I'm frightened of overdoing it with him."

"I think you're wrong, Mr McCain," said Billy. "You just don't realise the power here. I don't think you can overdo it with this horse. He just gets better and better. You should let him run at Ayr in a couple of weeks."

"That's three and a half miles, Billy. It's a really long one."

"I know. They'll be able to see something of his enormous stamina, then, won't they?"

"Mmm – I'd have to think about finding him a suitable jockey. Tommy Stack's already booked for that race. Actually, it's about time Red had his own permanent jockey. I want someone quiet. He's a sensitive animal, this one, and it must be someone he'll get on with."

He got back into the land-rover and started up the engine. Just before he moved off, he leant out of the window. "I think I've got it, Billy. I've just thought of the right person."

"Who?"

"Fletcher," shouted Mr McCain. "Brian Fletcher. He's already ridden one winner in the National, and from what I've heard about him, he's more chatty with his horses than he is with people."

It was not until Billy led me into the paddock at Ayr that I caught my first sight of Brian Fletcher. He looked very young and schoolboy-ish and he didn't say much either to me or Mr McCain. He just climbed into the saddle and we began to circle the paddock. I relaxed. I felt comfortable with him at once. I knew that this was the sort of jockey who would travel with me, letting me do things my own way.

"Do your best, lad," called Mr McCain. Whether he was speaking to me or to Brian, I was not sure. "If we get this one it will be five in a row."

"And if we don't, it'll be me that they blame," muttered Brian, as he trotted me round. "Well," he said aloud. "He certainly seems to be in fantastic shape. Most horses would be whacked after five races in six weeks."

"Not our Red," called Mr McCain. "You'll see – the more he runs, the better he goes. He positively flourishes on it."

"I hope you're right, Ginger," said a man standing nearby. "I've put my money on him today."

I enjoyed running with Brian, for he was almost a part of the saddle, quietly unobtrusive, yet ready to guide me if necessary. We zoomed round the course and finished easily, a full six lengths ahead of our pursuers.

Even the excitement of winning appeared to have little effect on him. When the press reporters flocked round, Brian just carried on undoing my girths and ignored them.

"What's the programme now, Mr McCain?" The questions came thick and fast.

"A little break now," said Mr McCain. "He's had a very heavy season so far. Then he goes to Liverpool for the National."

A reporter tapped Brian on the shoulder. "Would this do for Liverpool?"

Brian straightened up and surveyed the questioning faces. "This would do for me," he said very quietly, and walked off to the jockey's changing rooms.

When things had quietened down, he came to my stall and stood looking at me.

After a few minutes, Mr McCain looked up. "Oh, it's you, Brian. Well, what do you think of him?"

Brian's serious face suddenly broke into a grin. "I'm quite overcome with him. This is a typical Grand National horse. If you do run him in the National, I would love to ride him."

I looked at Mr McCain hopefully.

"We'll see, Brian. I'll let you know, after he's had a break."

Our mid-season rest consisted of nothing more strenuous than a walk along the seashore and gentle, daily exercise over the sand-dunes. It was good to have a break, but by the time that Christmas and the New Year were over I was beginning to feel restless. I was missing my gallops and both Glen and I were glad when the time came to begin serious training again. Now everything we did was aimed at our one main target – the Grand National at Aintree.

In January and February, all racetracks are completely at the mercy of the weather, and Mr McCain knew, by this time, that I was no good at all on soft and muddy ground. That sort of going was a far greater handicap than any weights I might have to carry in my saddle.

Once again, I delighted in my good fortune at being close to the sands, where the going never alters. Whatever the weather, I could enjoy my sand-gallops and both Glen and I spared a thought for our fellow 'chasers, who, all over the country, would be toiling through the thick February mud.

We had, by then, got the Annual Horror over with.'

'What on earth is the Annual Horror?' interrupted Andy.

Despite the warmth of the sunshine, Rummie shuddered. 'Clipping, Andy, I'll never get used to it, I'm afraid. I play up like mad, and they all dread it as much as I do. It's the one thing that drives me crazy. It takes them half a day to do Glen, and two weeks to get me finished, because I'll only let them do a bit at a time.'

Andy looked puzzled. 'Clipping? What's clipping, Rummie? I don't know what you mean.'

'They have to clip off our winter coats – with shears. I just can't bear the noise and the feel of those whirring blades against my skin. When I see my hair cascading to the floor I go berserk. They've tried everything, from cotton wool in my ears to a transistor radio to distract me, but it's no good. They always end up fleeing from my box until I've calmed down again.'

Andy, who had been listening in dumbstruck silence, finally found his voice. 'You mean that they cut off your winter coat, after you've gone to all the trouble of growing it? What on earth do they want to do a thing like that for? Don't they realise it's to help to keep you warm?' Andy looked so upset that Rummie began to wish that he had never mentioned the unpleasant subject of clipping.

'There is a very good reason for it, Andy – they don't just do it to torment us, you know. It's something that we all have to go through – those of us who work. It helps to prevent us from sweating too much. Working at the sort of pace we do when we're really building ourselves up in training, we would lose condition rapidly if we weren't clipped. It's unpleasant but very necessary, I'm afraid.'

'I'm surprised that you don't lose condition from the cold,' said Andy.

'We all wear stable rugs,' explained Rummie. 'Don't worry, they make sure that we're nice and cosy in the winter time.'

Andy tossed his head and sent three flies winging on their way. 'I'll never understand. It still sounds ridiculous to me. First they cut off your coat, causing you a great deal of upset in the process, then they cover you with something they've made specially to keep you warm. I prefer my way, thank you all the same. I cast off my winter coat when I'm good and ready, a bit at a time, and even then, it does someone else a bit of good. It's not just wasted, like yours is.'

Now it was Rummie's turn to look surprised. 'How's that, Andy?'

'Come over here and I'll show you,' said Andy mysteriously.

Rummie followed him across the field. Andy began to make his way slowly along the hedgerow, pausing occasionally to peer among the leafy upper branches. After a few minutes, he found what he was looking for.

'Here, Rummie,' he whispered. 'Be very quiet, though.'

Rummie pressed his nose into the midst of the hedge and looked down. For a moment, he could see nothing within the shadowy green foliage, and then, as his eyes adjusted to the dimness, he spotted the empty nest, a hollow, mossy cup. The inside had been painstakingly lined with Andy's coarse grey hairs, each one carefully woven into the mossy structure. In the lower branches, breast still brown-speckled, fluttered a young robin. He watched them and his eyes shone like two tiny black beads.

Andy looked at his friend proudly. 'There are three this time,' he whispered. 'All reared on my hair.'

Rummie looked at the robin, then at Andy, with amusement. Maybe that shaggy exterior did not conceal such a tough nut after all?

'Get on with your story, then,' said Andy, gruffly.

'Well it was hard work all the way then. I don't know which was worse, the build-up or the count-down to The Day. I had three more races to prepare me, and for the last two the ground was against me – too soft. I hated it, struggling round the track as best I could, feeling thoroughly miserable as the rain lashed into me.

But we couldn't afford to hang about waiting for the weather to improve, not at that late stage. We had just twenty-eight days left to complete our training programme, and when you're that near to the goal of a lifetime even the elements can't be allowed to intervene. Everyone realised that the bad weather was against me, and no one was too worried about my performances.

Mr McCain was delighted with the predictions of the racing press and came out to read something which evidently pleased him. "Billy, listen to this from *Chaseform Notebook*. 'Red Rum ran a great race on ground that was all against him. When the ground dries up he will be winning again'."

"We know that," said Billy, scornfully. "Let's hope that's one prediction that will come true. All we need now is an early spring, and we've really got everything going for us."

For the next few days, we did nothing more strenuous than hack about in the sand-dunes, and then Glen and I went straight back into hard training.

We both knew that the next two weeks were absolutely vital. The sort of mileage we were now covering, first at a canter, and then galloping, was enormous and as the days passed I got better and better. I had never felt so powerful in my life.

The rains finally ceased and the weather suddenly grew milder. We could sense the approaching spring at last, and I felt that even the weather was giving me her blessing. Everything was quite perfect and I determined that nothing was going to stop me now.

I felt more sure than any of them. Mr McCain and Brian Fletcher were hopefully confident, but poor Billy was the one that I felt sorry for. As the day grew nearer, his nerves became steadily worse and he was practically living in my box with me, terrified that something might go wrong. He fussed around me like a mother hen. Had I eaten up all my feed? Had I had enough – or too much? Was I suddenly going to be stricken down with colic? What if I went lame at the last minute?

Each time that he came to my box he would stare at me in relief, as if he thought that I might have been spirited away while his back was turned. No one suffered like poor Billy during that final week. I knew he was torturing himself, letting his imagination run riot amongst the most ghastly improbabilities, but there was nothing I could do to

*The 1975 Grand National: Red Rum and L'Escargot jump together,
but this time L'Escargot wins.*

ease his worries, and each day he could feel me growing more and
more powerful beneath him.

"He frightens me to death," he confessed to Mr McCain. "You just
wouldn't believe the way he's built up this week. I feel as if he's
going to run away with me – I had my feet right up to his ears before I
could pull him up that time." His voice broke with emotion. "What a
horse. I wouldn't miss it for the world, Mr McCain, but the responsibility terrifies me. When I think of all those thousands of punters,
and here am I, responsible for a Grand National favourite. I get the
shivers every time I think about it."

Mr McCain smiled. "Then don't think about it, Billy. Don't let
yourself go to pieces now. There's only tomorrow to get through, the

final gallops and then it's not up to you any more." He paused and then continued, slightly bemused. "Come to think of it, after tomorrow, it isn't up to me any more, either." He patted my neck. "One more day, Red, and then it's just you and Brian Fletcher – but mainly you. You'll be out there on your own, boy."

I tossed my head towards him, trying to let him know that I would not let them down.

Early on Friday morning, Glen and I set off for our final and vitally important work-out. Today had to be just right. Too much work and we'd be over the top, spoilt for tomorrow. Not enough, and we'd be setting off for Aintree 'underdone.' Mr McCain stared at us thoughtfully. If one had to make a choice, it was always safer to leave a horse underdone. When we arrived at the beach, it was unusually crowded, despite the early hour. Small knots of people clustered along the edges of the sand-dunes.

"Oh, no," muttered Billy. "We've got an audience."

Mr McCain came over to us. "I didn't dare to tell you before, because I didn't want you worrying, but there's a television crew here. They're going to film the final gallops. I've told them to keep well out of your way, so just pretend they don't exist. They don't matter, Billy. All that matters is you and the horses. I'll be here, watching and listening. Off you go."

Glen and I flew past the groups of onlookers, ignoring everything except the wind and the sea and the sand beneath us. The seagulls screamed and the sound of my hooves thudded in my ears.

I settled down into my pace and nothing else mattered, not even tomorrow. Every fibre was immersed in that moment. It was wonderful to know that I was achieving absolute perfection in that gallop, running wild and free in the place I most loved. When we returned to Mr McCain, my happiness seemed to transmit itself to him. He looked me over with shining eyes. I stamped restlessly – I longed to repeat the gallop.

"He's raring to go again," said Billy. "I can feel him building up."

Mr McCain bit his lip, perplexed. "I'm that scared of overdoing him, Billy. I'd never forgive myself if we spoiled him for tomorrow."

"Trust Red, Mr McCain. He's not daft – he knows better than any of us how far he can go."

Mr McCain nodded. "All right, Billy. Take him down again."

This time, I tested myself. This was my last chance to see how far I could stretch myself, to sound the depths of what my body could offer. Would it really meet the challenge that our ambition was going to make upon it?

When we got back, Mr McCain looked worried. "I think we've gone too far, Billy. I must have been mad to let him go again. No one puts that sort of work into a horse the day before a race like the National."

For the first time for weeks, Billy looked happy. The relief of having got the final gallops over with gave him new confidence. "Don't you worry, Mr McCain. He's just right now – I can tell. We've done it. This horse is ready for tomorrow."

He walked me back quietly, over the dunes and through the streets of Birkdale. Everywhere, people were rushing, racing to their shops and offices. Only Billy and I were at peace. Our work was over. Silently, we crossed the railway track, picked our way carefully between the second-hand cars that lined the forecourt and passed down the narrow alleyway which led us home.

We both knew that the next time I set out from that yard it would be the beginning of the biggest journey of my life.'

Chapter Twelve

THE COURSE

It was Aintree, Liverpool, on the morning of Saturday, March 31st, 1973. Brian Fletcher stood in front of the empty stands and looked at his watch. It was still early – another five nerve-racking hours to get through. Suddenly, viciously, he drove the heel of his boot into the ground. Good, the going was nice and firm, just as Red Rum loved it. He bent down and patted the damaged turf back into place before setting off on the long trudge round the course.

As he walked, he tried to plan his race – like a campaign. At each fence he paused, and memories of his two previous Nationals flooded back as he looked over each of the obstacles that they would encounter.

At least Red Rum would have a jockey who knew exactly what they were embarking on – two circuits which covered four and a half miles and no less than thirty difficult and daunting fences. This race was not like the Derby, all over in about three minutes. If you were in the National you struggled on for a full ten minutes that seemed like your whole lifetime – that is, if you made it to the end. This year there were to be thirty-eight runners. How many, Brian wondered, would finish the race?

He followed the course, which begins with a straight line of six fences running to the north-east. How smart they all looked, neatly dressed with spruce, fir and gorse, in readiness for the great race. By half past three that afternoon, they would resemble a battlefield.

At the sixth fence, he stopped. This was the notorious Becher's Brook, a 4' 10" (1.47 m) thorn fence, now dressed in readiness with a mantel of spruce and fir. How would Red Rum cope with that? It

88

would certainly be a test of his intelligence, as well as his ability, thought Brian, remembering that view of the far side from mid-air. How the stomach lurches when one suddenly sees the brook and the unexpected 5′ 6″ (1.67 m) drop down!

Beyond Becher's, he paused and looked back down the line of fences, towards the distant stands, and was overawed at the sheer immensity of the course. It was difficult to believe that this section was only one-fifth of the distance and fences to be covered.

He walked on towards the Canal Turn, carefully weighing the demands of the right-angle turn which immediately follows the fence itself, and would take them on to Valentine's Brook. Six more fences and then The Chair – the biggest one of all. Red Rum would have to jump a six-foot-wide ditch (1.8 m), followed by an enormous 5′ 2″ (1.57 m) high fence.

After the Chair comes the Water Jump. This, perhaps, would be even more treacherous, because a low and seemingly easy 2′ 6″ (.76 m) hedge-fence conceals a vast 12′ 6″ (3.8 m) spread of water beyond. In order to clear it, Red Rum would have to jump an overall length of 14′ 9″ (4.5 m).

Assuming that they managed to negotiate that first circuit successfully, they would then go round again, passing the stands, take fourteen of the fences for the second time – mercifully, the Chair and the Water Jump would not be included in the second circuit – and then into the 494 yards (450 m) of run-in to the winning post. At this point, Aintree would exact her final toll. Over the last few hundred yards, the ground begins to rise. It is not called Heartbreak Hill for nothing.

There was no doubt about it, thought Brian. Any horse who managed to finish that course would have demonstrated more than his ability and stamina – he would have proved his outstanding courage. The chances of even completing the course were about four to one against.

Red Rum was careful, dedicated and courageous. What more could any jockey ask for?

'Luck,' Brian said aloud. 'About seventy-five per cent of luck. That's what we're all asking for.'

THE GRAND NATIONAL COURSE
4 Miles 856 Yards

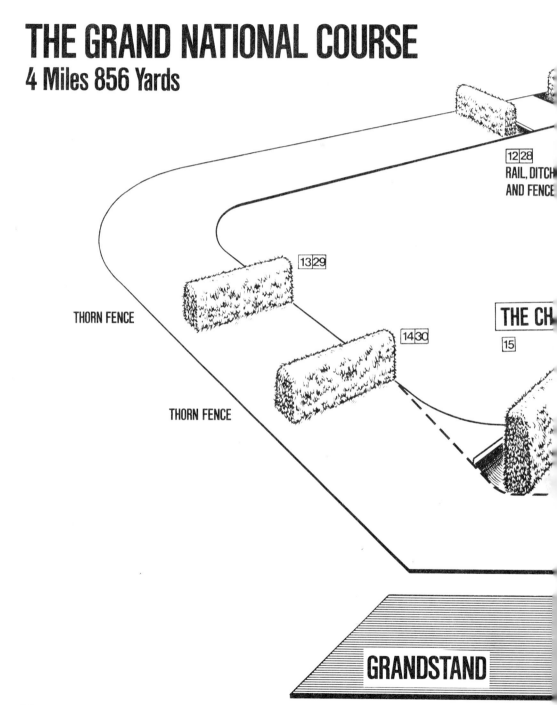

12 28
RAIL, DITCH
AND FENCE

13 29

THORN FENCE

14 30

THE CH

15

THORN FENCE

GRANDSTAND

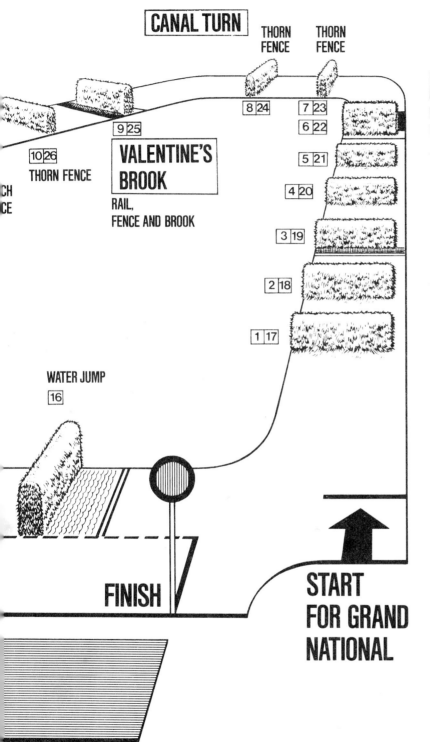

CANAL TURN

THORN FENCE

THORN FENCE

BECHER'S BROOK

RAIL, FENCE AND BROOK

THORN FENCE

THORN FENCE

8 24

7 23

6 22

9 25

5 21

VALENTINE'S BROOK

4 20

10 26

RAIL, FENCE AND BROOK

THORN FENCE

3 19

RAIL, DITCH AND FENCE

CH
CE

2 18

THORN FENCE

1 17

THORN FENCE

WATER JUMP

16

FINISH

START FOR GRAND NATIONAL

Chapter Thirteen

A DREAM COMES TRUE

'As they loaded Glenkiln and me into the transporter for our short journey to Aintree, it seemed, for a moment, almost unreal. Was it really only just over a year ago that I was crippled with that awful bone disease? Or was what was happening now only a dream, a horse's fairy tale from which I would suddenly and rudely awaken?

Jackie revved the engine and I braced myself as we began to move off. As always when I travel, I listened to the conversation up front.

"What d'you reckon then, Jackie?"

"Billy, stop worrying, will you? There's enough tension around here to light a match, without you getting the jitters."

"Well, how d'you expect me to feel? He's never seen Aintree. Mind you, he's clever enough to keep out of trouble. If something should happen to him . . ."

"Give over, Billy. You know what Tommy Stack said about him. That horse will look after himself. It's up to him, now."

Glen and I were settled into the racecourse stables, where we rested, glad of this time in which to compose ourselves. An hour before the race was due to begin, Billy and Jackie came back to us. The terrible hour of preparation and pre-race nerves had arrived.

"Good luck, Glen," I whispered.

"And to you, Rummie," said Glen. "I know you're going to do it."

"Don't say that, Glen. We can't both win, you know. You must look after yourself – we all must, now."

Those last moments were almost unbearable. Billy fumbled about, all fingers and thumbs, and the air reeked with a terrible nervous, sweating tension. It was hard not to let oneself be affected by it, and it was a great relief when we were finally led out into the paddock.

A seething mass of eyes stared at me as we began to circle. I heard my name over the loudspeakers: "Now opening at joint favourite, at 9–1, together with that mighty Australian horse, Crisp, comes Number 8, Red Rum. Ridden by Brian Fletcher, who is wearing the second colours of owner Noel Le Mare. And now, following Red Rum, and also from the McCain stables, Glenkiln. Glenkiln is ridden by newcomer Jonjo O'Neill, who is today wearing Mr Le Mare's first colours."

We did another circuit of the paddock, and then we stopped for a moment in front of Mr Le Mare. The old man looked from Glen to me, and someone took his arm. "Come on, Noel, you must leave yourself plenty of time to get back to the stands."

Although he was very pale, he looked at us both with bright, sharp eyes. "Have a safe journey," he said. "Come back safe and sound."

He turned to the crowd at his elbow. "Remember Devon Loch," he cautioned. In the 1956 National, Devon Loch was within a few yards of the winning post. The roar of the crowd, expecting him to win, distracted the horse, and as he relaxed his concentration his legs splayed out beneath him. The excitement of the crowd had robbed him of his victory. "Red Rum is a Liverpool horse," Mr Le Mare went on. "Half Liverpool and half Southport will be on him. Keep quiet until he's past the winning post – please."

Mr McCain stepped forward. "Right, Brian, this is it, then. You've got it planned?"

Brian nodded. "I'm going to try and stay out of trouble on the first circuit, get him nicely settled into the race. Once we're over the Chair, we'll start to take the field and give them a real race – a jockey's race. The main thing, first time round, will be to try and dodge the fallers."

We lined up. Thirty-eight names, thirty-eight hopes, and a strange hush now replaced the noise and bustle that had been steadily mounting throughout the day. The starter gave his signal and, as the field leapt forward, the loudspeaker crackled overhead.

I resisted the temptation to plunge straight into the thick of it. Brian steered me to the outside and we kept to the middle of the field.

After the fourth fence, Crisp, my joint favourite, took the lead.

"Wait." Brian restrained me and as we careered down the track the obstacles came so fast that I could allow nothing to distract me, not even for a second. Nothing else existed now. There was only my race and the persistent man-chant that accompanied it. We sailed over Becher's, oblivious of those who fell. I could hear nothing but the pounding of my hooves and heart, and that feverish, almost hysterical, chant from the loudspeakers:

". . . Crisp, well clear, over from Grey Sombrero who jumps it second, Endless Folly jumps it third, then Great Noise fourth – five is Black Secret, six is Rouge Autumn, seven is Spanish Steps and eight is Tarquin Bid and nine is Red Rum. Ten, on the outside, is Sunny Lad as they come up to the next . . ."

We floated over the fourteenth fence like a dream. I was really warmed up, now and beginning to enjoy myself.

". . . Crisp over in the lead and clear . . . Red Rum well in there and then comes Glenkiln. Coming to the Chair now – this is the biggest. Crisp, ears pricked, jumps it beautifully in the lead – he just pecked a little bit, but got away with it. Grey Sombrero's gone at that one. Grey Sombrero's a faller, Glenkiln's a faller . . ."

I pushed away the wave of concern immediately. Worrying about Glen would only hold me back. Now I was the only one left for them to hope for. Ignoring my friend's distress was, perhaps, the toughest discipline of all.

Carefully, I cleared the enormous width of the Water Jump and we thundered on past the remnants of the field and into the second, vital circuit. Away ahead, Crisp was already disappearing, and we were in second place, a long way back.

". . . Crisp at the ditch, the nineteenth – he stood right back, he jumped it well, he's right out in front still of Red Rum, Rouge Autumn is third, Spanish Steps fourth . . ."

The voice changed as another commentator took over:

". . . And Richard Pitman over that one on Crisp and what a fantastic ride he's having! I can't remember a horse so far ahead in the Grand National at this stage. Jumping that second was Red Rum, then Spanish Steps on the outside of Rouge Autumn, Great Noise made a mistake there, but coming up to the next . . . Crisp is over it safely, from Red Rum, Crisp comes on his own to Becher's Brook for the second time, Crisp, the top weight. Richard Pitman over it in tremendous style and he's about twenty lengths clear from Red Rum in second place . . ."

I can't be second, I thought. Not all this to be second.

At that moment, Brian shouted at me, "Come on, Red. We're not going to settle for second, come on!"

I quickened and we began to gain ground as I drew upon the reserves of strength that I had been saving. They were really needed now, and I only hoped there was enough left in me.

". . . two left to jump and it's Crisp with Red Rum in second place making ground, but a very long gap after that to Hurricane Rock, Spanish Steps and Rouge Autumn. . ."

On we thundered, and another voice took over the commentary:

". . . It's Crisp in the lead from Red Rum, but Red Rum is *still* making ground on him! Brian Fletcher on Red Rum chasing Dick Pitman on Crisp. Crisp still well clear with two fences left to jump in the 1973 National and this great Australian 'chaser Crisp, with twelve stone on his back, and ten stone five on the back of Red Rum . . . who's chasing him and they look to have it absolutely to themselves. At the second last – Crisp is over and clear of Red Rum, who's jumping it a long way back. In third place is Spanish Steps, then Hurricane Rock and Rouge Autumn and L'Escargot. But coming up to the final fence in the National, now . . . and it's Crisp still going great – he jumps it well. Red Rum is about fifteen lengths behind him as he jumps it. Dick Pitman coming up to the elbow now in the National. He's got two hundred and fifty yards left to run – but Crisp is just wandering off the true line now. He's beginning to lose concentration. He's been out there on his own for too long. And Red Rum is making ground on him."

I knew that Crisp could hear me coming. For the first time in over four miles, he could hear the sound of hooves that were not his own.

He raced onwards, valiantly, but I could tell that he was exhausted. I prayed that the winning line would not come too soon, for inch by inch I was closing the gap. Now a new strength and power thrust me on, and it seemed to come from my mind rather than my body.

". . . Still, as they come to the line, it's a furlong to run now, two hundred yards now for Crisp and Red Rum still closing in on him, and Crisp is getting very tired and Red Rum is pounding after him and Red Rum is the one who finishes strongest. *He's going to get up! Red Rum is going to win the National!* At the line, Red Rum has just *snatched* it from Crisp! *And Red Rum is the winner!* And Crisp is second and L'Escargot is just coming up to be third . . ."

I heard no more. The roar of the crowd, now on its feet, seemed to swallow us up, blotting out even the thunder of my own heart. By the final lunge of a head, I had just turned the dreams of a lifetime into reality.

Just like the tide, the crowd surged towards us and it became impossible to move, and then Billy and Jackie were at my head, leading me forward towards Mr Le Mare and Mr McCain. Two police horses closed in to escort us, and, above the din, the loudspeakers made an announcement:

"Red Rum has just smashed the Grand National record time – a record that has remained unbeaten since the year 1934, when Golden Miller completed the course in 9 minutes 20 seconds. Today, Red Rum took just 9 minutes 1.9 seconds – an average speed of 29 miles per hour over the biggest obstacles in Britain."

Billy looked at Jackie, too full to speak. Behind me, I knew, came Crisp, and I felt sorry for him. He had run a great race, burdened with top weight, only to have victory snatched from him at the final moment. We continued to make our way slowly through the surging mob and then, suddenly, above the uproar, I heard the sound of a distant shot. As I started, Billy held me tightly. Jackie looked at him questioningly.

"Grey Sombrero," said Billy quietly. "He didn't make it."

Eventually, they got me into the transporter. Glen was already there, all tucked up and very miserable.

As soon as the doors were closed, I turned to him. "Glen, are you all right? What happened?"

"I don't want to talk about it," said Glen stiffly. "Not at the moment, if you don't mind. Don't you go bothering about me. This is your day. See that you enjoy it. It's much too precious to waste."

Beyond the doors, the crowd were still shouting and cheering. They began to chant my name – I was their new hero. Jackie kept sounding the horn and flashing the headlights and eventually we began to move, in slow convoy, behind Mr McCain's car. Reluctantly, the crowd parted to let us through. It was cool and dim inside the stall. For the first time in hours, my mind stopped racing and I had chance to think.

Victory on this scale did not feel quite as I had imagined. During the afternoon, I had become aware of something that had never previously occurred to me.

How many more Glens were now journeying painfully home? There had been a lot of men, and a lot of good horses, involved in that race. They had all, by being there, made a contribution towards my moment of glory. My triumph meant sadness and defeat for the rest, and I have never forgotten what either of those things feels like.

My success was their failure and winning was lonely, after all. I turned to look at poor Glen and then I realised what he had meant. He was right – this glory was a privilege. Not to enjoy it would be nothing less than ingratitude.

I always know when we turn in to Aughton Road. I've made the journey so many times that I know the sounds, the stops and starts. I braced myself as we went round the final corner. Another couple of minutes, and we'd be home. Suddenly, Jackie braked, then I heard the voice of Mr McCain. Jackie wound down the window. "What's up, Guv?"

"The road's blocked, Jackie. At first, I thought there had been an accident. There are police cars all over the place and the street's jammed."

"What's going on?" asked Billy.

Mr McCain grinned from ear to ear, and waved his hand towards me. "It's the crowd, lads. They're waiting for him – for all of us."

A police car pulled alongside. "We'll escort you, Sir," said the driver.

"Thank you" said Mr McCain. "Billy, when we get there, take him up and down the road for a bit, then the people can see him. Jackie and I will get poor Glen round to his box. He's taken a terrible bashing. It almost chokes me to see him so stiff and sore. He's such a good-hearted horse."

When we finally managed to get back to the yard, there was not a cobble to be seen. Our little haven of peace had been transformed.

Now it was a seething mass of excited, celebrating people. When Billy did, at last, manage to get me into my box, I suddenly felt terribly tired. I watched for a while. Our tiny yard was overflowing with locals and neighbours and strangers and champagne. Cameras flashed, toasts were drunk and the joyful celebrations went on and on. My eyes grew heavy and then they began to close. The noises faded and I fell into a deep, peaceful sleep. I think I'd earned that rest.'

Chapter Fourteen

ENJOYING FAME

'I think we both need a rest after that,' said Andy, and promptly lowered himself to the ground. Carefully, he folded back one foreleg to create a chin-rest. 'Come on, Rummie, relax. It exhausts me just listening to you, when you go on like that.'

Rummie cropped the grass for a few minutes before lying down beside his friend. The sky told him that it was already late afternoon. The summer was well advanced now, and even his quiet stretch of beach would have its fair share of holiday-makers. There would be deck-chairs and ice-creams and children. He liked children. They would be building sandcastles over his gallops, clambering over the dunes and paddling along the shoreline, just as he did.

All at once, he felt restless. Reliving the race had stirred all the old excitement and now he was looking forward to the next season. It was the same every year. Such a tremendous relief to have conquered Aintree, to allow himself to wind down, and then, a few weeks later, ambition would begin to reproach him.

He glanced at Andy, who was fast asleep. How could he bear to spend season after season, year after year, mooching about in that same field? Never to know anything different?

'I suppose that's what donkeys are all about,' he thought. 'They're there to calm you down.'

He got up suddenly. Andy opened one eye. 'Rummie?' he murmured sleepily. 'Where are you going?'

'Just for a wander. Do you want to come?'

Andy began to struggle to his feet and after a few tries his hind legs finally co-operated. He shook himself awake. 'Get a bit stiff nowadays.'

'How old are you, Andy?'

'I'm not quite sure, to be honest. I think I can give you a few years. You don't have birthdays if you haven't got a pedigree. One year is much the same as another, except for this one, of course . . .' He stopped, embarrassed by his slip of the tongue.

'It's all right, Andy,' said Rummie gently. 'This year has been different for me, too.'

They wandered up the hedgerow together, sometimes pausing to bite off a stem of lacy cow-parsley from the base of the hedge.

'I think they'll be coming to get me soon,' said Rummie. 'It's time I got back into training.'

'You can't go yet. You haven't finished the story, have you?'

'Not quite,' replied Rummie, 'but since the first National obviously wore you out, I've no intention of delving into all of them. I don't want to turn into the Great Grand National Bore.'

Andy stared at him. 'Rummie, you'll never be that. You might wear me out, but you'll never be boring.'

Just then, their conversation was interrupted by a car turning into the drive. Andy looked questioningly as several people, some with cameras, emerged and clustered round the gate. Rummie's attention was riveted upon the newcomers.

Their voices floated across the paddock: 'There he is – that's him.' 'What a fantastic looking horse. So alert – just look at that stance. He really knows there's something going on.'

One of the men detached himself from the group as Mrs Wareing appeared from the bungalow. 'Good afternoon, you are expecting us, aren't you? We arranged to take a few photographs for our magazine.'

'Oh, yes, we've been expecting you,' said Mrs Wareing.

As the introductions progressed, Andy nosed at Rummie impatiently.

'What's going on?' he demanded.

'Keep cool, Andy. It's only the press. Don't you worry. I'll handle this. I'm used to it. It's great fun. I didn't expect them to turn up here, though, I must say. They'll probably want to take your picture, too.'

Andy stared at Rummie unbelievingly. 'What on earth for? They must be crazy – no one comes around taking *my* picture.'

'You'd better get used to it quickly, then. Whether you like it or not, you'll probably be billed as my Summer Companion.'

Andy looked annoyed. 'I've never heard such nonsense in my life. Summer Companion, indeed! Sounds like the name of a flower.'

'Now don't you start getting difficult,' Rummie warned. 'They love this sort of thing and I quite enjoy it myself. They've probably travelled miles for this. Don't let them down, Andy. Just relax and let me deal with it.'

And deal with it he did. Andy looked on in amazement. This was a side of his friend he had not seen before. Although he disapproved, he could not help admiring Red Rum the Showman.

Rummie began by standing his ground, alert, questioning and excited. The cameras flashed.

A smartly dressed lady leaned over the gate, holding out a carrot. 'Rummie,' she called, in a high, clear voice. 'Come on, Rummie, there's a lovely boy.'

'Go right into the field, darling,' said one of the cameramen. 'I want a shot of him approaching you.'

'I can't go in there,' she retorted indignantly. 'You know I'm frightened to death of horses.'

'Red will be fine with you,' said Mrs Wareing. 'He's very gentle, there's nothing to worry about.'

'But he's so big,' protested the lady and turned imploring eyes on her friend. 'Can't you photograph me with the donkey? Such a sweet little donkey, much more my size.'

Andy glared, first in the direction of the lady, and then at Rummie. 'Any more of this stuff, and my back legs will be getting restless,' he muttered.

'Shut up and behave yourself,' Rummie ordered. 'Just graze casually for a couple of minutes.'

The lady tried again. 'Rummie – carrots. Come along.'

Andy began to pull the grass. 'That's a bit familiar. "Rummie" indeed! You're not really going over there, are you?'

'Of course I am,' Rummie told him. 'I wouldn't let them down, you should know me better than that.'

Reluctantly, the lady clambered over the gate and Mrs Wareing pressed a packet of mints into her hand.

'Right,' said Rummie. 'This is it.' His legs jerked into action and he flew across the grass. The lady shrank back.

'Stay there – don't move,' called Mrs Wareing. 'You'll be all right.'

Rummie careered towards the lady, hoping that she would not fail them both, and the cameras flashed.

'Give him a mint, dear,' the cameraman called. 'I want a shot of him taking a mint from you.'

As the lady fumbled with the packet, Rummie looked down at the group, haughtily. He wished the lady would relax. It was always easier to have a bit of fun when people were at their ease. He tossed his head towards Andy. 'Come on, you miserable moke. Don't be such a spoil-sport.' Andy shuffled over, taking a long time about it, and glared crossly at the lady before accepting the mint she held out.

'You are absolutely hopeless,' whispered Rummie, and began nosing enthusiastically towards the packet. His audience were delighted, and even the lady began to smile. Rummie continued to demand peppermints long after the packet was finished, and Andy grew impatient.

'Come on, Rummie – pack it in.'

'Not likely. I'm going to chase you off in a minute. Just run a few yards into the field and begin to graze. They'll call me back again, but you don't need to get involved.'

'Oh, look – you can tell who's the boss around here,' laughed the lady as Andy shambled thankfully away. 'Poor little donkey, does he always get bullied like that?'

Mrs Wareing shook her head. 'Not really, they get on very well together. I think Red's just asserting himself because you're here.'

Rummie came back to the gate, made a great show of sniffing for non-existent peppermints and then moved briskly over to the water trough.

'Look, he's thirsty now,' remarked the lady.

Obediently, the whole team moved over to the trough and watched as Rummie embarked upon his grande finale. He lowered his nose

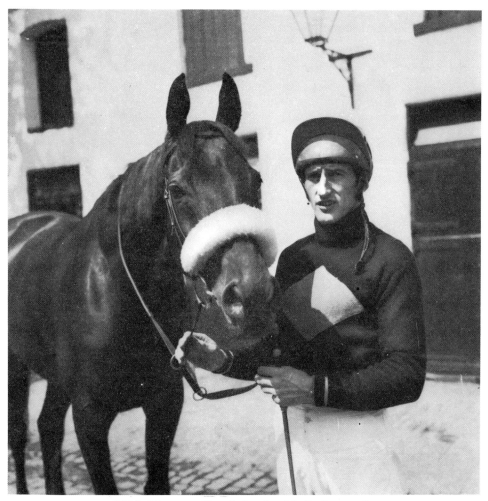

With Tommy Stack in the McCain yard.

into the water, and then, instead of drinking, he began to flip his upper lip backwards and forwards vigorously, until the whole surface rippled. When he was satisfied that he had created sufficient movement, he lifted his muzzle until it was just level with the water. Skilfully flexing his upper lip, he covered himself with a shower of droplets. 'Oh, just look at that,' someone shouted. 'I've never seen a horse do that before. He's wetting himself through.' Rummie raised his lovely eyes towards them, lifted his nose a fraction higher, and blew, hard. As the mini-shower cascaded in their midst, the little group jumped backwards.

'He's done it on purpose – I'm sure he has,' someone shouted. 'He's sending us up.'

Well satisfied, Rummie tossed his wet nose heavenwards, shook the final glistening drops over the party and busily returned to his grazing as the handkerchiefs appeared.

'You are an awful show-off, Rummie,' said Andy, after the people had gone.

'I know,' Rummie replied, between mouthfuls of grass. 'But people love it – they expect it of me. I'd be very upset if you thought I was like that with my own kind.'

Andy thought about that for a moment. 'No, I don't think you are. Not from what I know about you, anyway. I suppose I'd be terribly conceited if I'd achieved a fraction of your record.'

Rummie smiled. 'Yes – you're bad enough as it is. You mustn't take this people thing too seriously, Andy. It's just a bit of fun. I do a lot of public appearances now and I can hardly let them down by just walking around like a snooty old thoroughbred. Not when they've all turned out to see me. You have to horse around a bit, if you're parading at Southport Show, or switching on the Blackpool Illuminations.

'I enjoy it, I'm not ashamed to admit it, and it does make a nice change from the tensions of the racetrack. I find it very flattering, really, and I've no intention of letting my fans down.'

'What I really want to know,' said Andy, after thinking a while, 'is why you carried on after that first National. You had all achieved your ambition, all three of you, so why not leave it at that?

'I thought the National finished most horses, anyway. If you've done it, you've done it and hurrah. If you've done it and failed, you must never want to see that dreadful course again.'

'Well, I can see what you mean,' said Rummie, 'but you obviously don't understand what ambition is like. Ambition is what makes me tick. If you took that away from me – well, I'd only be half a horse.'

Andy wrinkled up his muzzle and gazed across the paddock. 'I don't know whether I ought to pity you, or envy you,' he said quietly. 'As it is, I don't do either of those things, but I can't help liking you.'

'Would you like to hear the rest?' asked Rummie.

Andy butted him, playfully. 'I won't let you go back into training until I have.'

Chapter Fifteen

SECOND TIME AROUND

'It was not until the next day that I realised how stiff and achy I felt. Fit as I was, I had overtaxed my muscles as never before. I had also, during the race, sustained a nasty, deep little cut which I had not even noticed at the time.

Compared with poor Glen, however, I was just fine. Even watching him was painful. When he had fallen at the Chair, he could not get up because his leg was stuck in the bottom of the fence. He lay there, struggling in the water and one of the other horses came over and caught him on the back of his head. He was so dazed, when he did finally get to his feet, that he doesn't even remember being led back to the stables.

For the next three days, we hobbled around in our boxes, like a pair of old wrecks, and then they came and took us to the place we most longed for.

The sea was like balm. It smelt good and it felt good. We just stood there, chest deep, and the waves lapped over us. Those lingering aches of Aintree vanished with the tide. As we passed through the streets, I soon discovered that I now basked in a blaze of glory. People stopped to look at us and motorists waited politely, often winding down their windows to call out greetings and congratulations.

"I never knew that Southport was such a horsy town," Jackie commented.

"It isn't," replied Billy, "but I guess our Red is just about the greatest celebrity they've ever had. And he knows it. There's something different about him now. Not haughty, exactly . . ."

"Regal," said Jackie. "He's this year's king and he intends to enjoy it. I don't blame him, either. That title was earned the hard way."

That was when I realised that I didn't want to be king for only one year. I had to go to Aintree again, I could not bear to think of them running the National without me. Now that I knew what it was all about, I would do even better. Next time I wanted to win easily, not just by a head.

This determination increased when I overheard someone telling Mr McCain that the Grand National finished most horses and would probably prove to have finished me. "Especially after beating the record time," said the visitor. "After a desperate set-to like he had with Crisp, you can't expect very much more from him."

From my box, I glared crossly at the man, but he was too busy talking to notice. "Even if it hasn't finished him off," this expert continued, "he'll need completely reschooling after those massive Aintree fences. He'll do no good on an ordinary course after Aintree."

"Then we'll reschool him," said Mr McCain. "Billy can take him over to the schooling paddock with a couple of lead horses."

When I saw those silly little hurdles that they were expecting me to go over, I was so annoyed that I just ducked out to one side. What an insult, Andy, taking me back to playschool! I stood there, looking so offended that Mr McCain and Billy burst out laughing.

"I think we've hurt his feelings, Billy."

"You can hardly blame him, Mr McCain. After Becher's and the Chair, he obviously considers this is kid's stuff. He'll be all right. I'm sure he knows best."

"Well, as long as he doesn't start considering ordinary courses beneath him as well," said Mr McCain. "I'm just a little worried that he's going to stand back and rest on his laurels now. It would be an awful shame. I'm sure he's got more to offer. I'd love to take him again, next year."

"You will," said Billy, confidently. "I know Red, his target will be exactly the same as yours – next year's National. He has got a lot of self-discipline, as long as we let him make his own rules. Reschooling evidently isn't a part of the schedule that he's mapped out for himself."

They watched anxiously during my next races, for Mr McCain was still afraid that Aintree might have soured me. Just to put his mind at rest, I decided it was time to really prove that I was going better than ever.

We were running at Carlisle, and the final run-in to the winning post is uphill, providing me with an excellent opportunity to show them something special. I thundered up, a good fifteen lengths ahead of the others and did not bother to stop. I just carried on past the winning post and disappeared round the bend, only sorry that I could not see their faces. Finally, Brian managed to stop me, and we cantered back.

"What happened, Brian? What's the matter?"

Brian Fletcher was laughing so much that he almost collapsed across my neck. "Nothing happened – I just couldn't pull the old devil up, that's all. He was running away with me; he refused to stop."

"I know the feeling," said Billy. "He's fantastic."

Brian nodded "You're right, no horse goes like that straight after Aintree."

Mr McCain stepped foward. "Then what do you say to us letting him challenge Crisp again? Just the two of them, at level weights, at the Doncaster meeting?"

I pricked up my ears. That would, indeed, be quite a challenge. Crisp had carried the maximum handicap of twelve stone, in the National, to my ten stone five pounds. If I went to Aintree again, I, too, would be saddled with that maximum handicap. I had great admiration for Crisp. After all, it was to him that I owed my record-beating performance. It had been Crisp, not I, who had set the pace that memorable day. The least I could do would be to meet him at level weights: to give him the opportunity to get his own back.

Brian Fletcher pursed his lips. "It's up to you, Mr McCain, but I think you may be being a little too ambitious. Crisp is quite a horse, you know."

"And so is Red Rum. It will be an interesting race." '

'What happened?' Andy asked.

Rummie champed the grass. 'He beat me,' he said ruefully. 'Crisp avenged himself for the National. He set a fantastic pace right from the start and he won by eight lengths. I just couldn't compete – I wasn't really at my best, that day. Poor Crisp went lame after the race and had to be retired for the rest of the season. Everyone at the yard was very crestfallen about my defeat, but in a way, it did us good. We'd all persuaded ourselves that I was now invincible and I think we needed to be taken down a couple of pegs. And I'm glad that it was Crisp who did it.

The year passed quickly and, almost before I realised, it was February again and we were into those strange, tense weeks which lead up to the highlight of the racing year.

Sometimes, the days flashed by so quickly that it seemed Aintree would be upon us before we were ready. The blacksmith came round to fit my special aluminium racing plates, which are so much lighter than our ordinary working shoes that they always feel strange to begin with.

As nerves grew steadily more frayed, our long trek towards the National seemed even harder than the race itself. It is the same every year.

Mr McCain and Billy took a special interest in the weather reports. They knew I could cope with the burden of being saddled with top weight in normal circumstances – but not if I had to carry it over soft, squelchy ground. Ten days before the race, the weather improved, and with each passing day the ground became firmer as it dried out. The sun shone at last, and Billy went over to Aintree to check the turf. His report was optimistic. "As long as the weather holds out, the going will be perfect for him – the turf's like silk at the moment."

That year, there was already a crowd waiting on the forecourt when

I was led out to the transporter. As I walked up the ramp, they began to cheer. I glanced back at them before Billy closed the doors. He patted me on the neck. "Don't worry, Red. There'll be more than that when we get home. You'll not let them down."

As we travelled to the course, I remembered how I had felt the first time. I had been so full of restless excitement that only my hopes and determination had held my fluttering nerves at bay.

It was different now. I had seen it all before. I knew exactly what that course was going to demand of me, and how Brian and I were going to cope with it. Having dedicated the last twelve months towards this day, I felt almost sorry that it would soon be over.

Once again, we circled the paddock before a crowd of curious, staring faces, and I overheard snatches of their conversation as I passed by.

"That's last year's winner."

"What are the chances of him doing it again?"

"No, not two years on the run – he only just managed it last time, you know. Hardly likely to have the same luck twice."

"How's the betting going? No, he's moved out of the betting, he's no longer favourite."

As I circled for the second time, still listening to those drifting voices, I smiled to myself. They did not seem to realise that I had worked for a whole year towards this moment, that I had got no more than ten hair-raising minutes in which to show them all something that they would never forget.

As we got into line, the sun shone down, warming my back as if giving me her blessing. The course unwound into the distance, empty and green and firm. Way off, I could see the first line of fences and I knew that beyond the far bend lay all the great challenges and sneaky pitfalls that my beloved Aintree had to offer.

Now I felt impatient to get round the first, chaotic, circuit, to work my way carefully through that dangerous jumble of fallers and loose horses and get past the stands again. It was then that I intended to make the second circuit my own.

After today, Aintree would really belong to me. I adored the challenge of this course and now I was going to take it by the throat.

The first time round was dangerous. There were a lot of riderless horses ploughing around in our midst and these were far more unnerving than any of the obstacles. When we came on past the stands again, there were only two horses in front. We were now well clear of the rest of the field and I knew that my moment had arrived.

I could settle down to enjoy myself at last and my hooves began to swallow up the ground. Brian stood up in the stirrups and began to pull me back with all his might. "Not yet, Red – save it!"

I could hear the commentator. He was getting very excited, and so was the crowd. I felt Brian relax again and knew that he had decided to leave the rest to me. I flew past the opposition and now the rest of the course lay ahead of me, as free and empty as the sand gallops.

As I danced over the turf in that warm sunshine, I was just beginning to think that the whole thing was almost too easy when I heard the thud of hooves getting closer. The loudspeaker informed me that L'Escargot was moving up to challenge me. Was he going to do to me as I had done to Crisp?

I flew on, over the final fence and began that last, uphill run to the winning post. The sounds of L'Escargot began to recede and were blotted out completely by the hysterical roaring of the crowd. Brian was so relaxed that he loosened his grip to wave to the crowd, even before we had crossed the line, and had to grab hold again quickly as he began to lose his balance.

I pulled up, and the ovation lapped around me.

"What a horse – what a horse!" Brian kept repeating, over and over. "He didn't need a jockey."

That year, I travelled home totally at peace with myself. Everything had happened just as I had intended, and I felt quite sad that I would have to wait a whole year before the next National. I had outgrown ordinary courses now. Only a Grand National held the glamour and excitement that I had come to love.'

Chapter Sixteen

THE KING OF AINTREE

'The following week, after we had finished galloping on the sands, Billy stood talking with Mr McCain.

"This should be a tired horse in need of a rest. Instead, he's fitter and stronger than ever. What are you going to do with him? I can't see him settling at grass yet, but I don't think he'd enjoy ordinary races, either. He's become very choosy now – he only likes Grand Nationals, and there aren't enough of those to keep him happy."

"There is one," said Mr McCain.

Billy stared at him. "You don't mean the Scottish National?"

Mr McCain nodded.

"But that's run in a fortnight's time."

Mr McCain nodded again. "I know what you're going to say, and so is everybody else. No horse has ever won two Nationals in the same year. No horse can recover from Aintree in only three weeks. It would be sheer madness to run him again so soon. Well, forget about everyone else, and all the criticisms, Billy. Just tell me honestly – what do you think?"

Billy looked at me thoughtfully, before he spoke. "I think he could do it, Mr McCain. The rules don't apply any longer, when you're talking about Red Rum, because he makes his own. I think we could give him the chance. If he did happen to win, he really would have immortalised himself."

I won the Scottish National by four lengths, and was rewarded with the ovation of my career. Someone even said that I wasn't really a horse, I was a miracle.'

Andy stared at his friend. He stood there, eyes shining, ears pricked, as if hearing again the applause and the cheering.

'I think that was my finest year, Andy. I'll never, ever forget it. In a way, it made up for the next two Nationals.'

'I can't understand how you came to lose those,' said Andy. 'You can't have been past your best, or you wouldn't have gone back and won again, so what went wrong?'

'Well, the third time I ran, the going was soft and I just can't give my best on that sort of ground. I really do hate it – it just wasn't the same for me, struggling round under those conditions, lumbered with top weight.

'L'Escargot won that time. It was an awful disappointment to come in second, but Mr McCain was very proud of me. He said that it was really a far greater achievement to come second, over ground that I loathed, than to have won the other two. A lot of horses wouldn't even have bothered to try, you know.'

'Yes, I can see that,' said Andy. 'And what about the next time – was the weather against you then?'

Rummie smiled. 'No, that year was different. The reasons are a bit more complicated, but the weather was not one of them.' He stopped talking and began to crop the grass.

'Go on, then,' said Andy impatiently. 'Don't stop now.'

'Well, I know why I didn't win, but I don't really know very much about the reasons that led up to the change.'

'What change?'

'The jockey change,' said Rummie. 'As you know, Brian Fletcher had been riding me for a long time by then, and we'd really got to know each other. Between us, we made a great team, as the results had already proved. I was used to him, and he respected my judgement completely. He always assumed that I knew best and let me have the upper hand, and it had always paid off handsomely.

'Anyway, for whatever reason, the partnership was suddenly dissolved. Perhaps Mr McCain thought that Brian was too easy-going with me, that we'd grown too used to each other, but I'm only guessing. For the 1976 Grand National, I was to have a new jockey, yet not so new after all. It's funny how paths continue to cross.'

'I think I can guess who it was,' Andy interrupted. 'Was it Mr Stack?'

'Right first time, Andy. Now Mr Stack and I have always respected each other, but he's quite a different sort of personality from Brian—much more dominant, and if it comes to a battle of wills between us, I'd be the one to give in. That is what happened in the '76 National. We had only got two fences left to jump and I was ready to thrust forward and take the field. Mr Stack held me back, and that is where I made by big mistake. I let him do it. I shouldn't have listened to him – not at that late stage. I knew best, and I've always regretted my weakness. Right at the end, Rag Trade overtook me. We could have been first, that year, not second. And right behind us, finishing third, came Brian Fletcher on a complete outsider called Eyecatcher.'

'It wasn't your fault,' said Andy comfortably. 'You can't go blaming yourself for it.'

Rummie trotted over to the water trough. 'There's no point in sorrowing over lost races – but it was my fault. I shouldn't have taken any notice. A good horse doesn't go around blaming his jockey, Andy. Mr Stack thought he was right. After all, it was the first time he had ridden me in the National, which is very different from any other race. I was the one who made the big mistake – I should have trusted my own judgement.

'Anyway, it was all the more reason why I had to go back this year and win. Mr Stack and I had grown used to each other's ways by then. The weather was perfect, the sun smiled and I set out with all the confidence in the world. It was that sort of morning, Andy – the

114   *Red Rum takes the last fence safely ahead of the field in the 1977 Grand National, to make history by becoming the first horse to win three times.*

moment they took me out of my box, I knew that it was going to be my day. I was relaxed and sure of myself again. That's the way to conquer Aintree, Andy. You just have to go on out there and swallow it up, and that is what I did. I became the only horse ever to win the Grand National three times. Aintree belongs to me now.'

After a few moments, Andy spoke. 'But for how long, Rummie? How long can you go on like this?'

Rummie looked down at his small friend. 'That's one question I never ask myself, Andy. Who knows? I'll be running again in '78. Maybe it will be my last time. If it is, I just hope that I can go out in a final blaze of glory. Even if I don't, I'll still have the satisfaction of knowing that it will take one giant of a horse to beat my record.

'I've come an awful long way from Rossenarra, and I've been so lucky. So many things have contributed towards my success. Sandra, then Southport and the sea – what more could any horse ask for?'

'I'm not going to let you say that,' said Andy firmly. 'It wasn't luck, Rummie. You did it – you made it all happen. Ambition can often be a vice – but courage is a great virtue, and when the two come together, the way they have in you, then miracles begin to happen. The rest of us can only stand back and watch.'

Rummie looked at the shaggy donkey in amazement. 'I can hardly believe my ears,' he gasped. 'Was that really you talking?'

Andy wrinkled his nose. 'Yes, it was, you old jockey-lover.'

Rummie lowered his head and charged. 'Holy Moke!' thought Andy and set off speedily for the shelter. When he was almost there, he turned round. Rummie was standing in the middle of the field, laughing. Andy shuffled back to him, kicked up the dry turf and sank down to enjoy a glorious, dusty old roll.

'That's the best idea you've had all day,' said Rummie, and joined his friend on the ground.

As the orange and cream transporter turned into the drive, Billy looked out of the window anxiously. 'Oh, Jackie – will you take a look at that?'

Red was down on the grass, in the middle of the most undignified roll. A few yards away, the shaggy grey donkey was indulging in exactly the same tactics.

'What a pair they make,' said Billy. 'It's almost a shame to separate them. Just look at Red, though. He's as fat as a pig. It's going to take weeks to get him really fit again. I don't think we've come a moment too soon.'

'I reckon you're going to have a bit of fun trying to catch him,' said Jackie, as he switched off the engine. 'I bet that scruffy donkey's been a rotten influence on him.'

Billy shook his head. 'Not if I know my Red. Being at grass is all very well for a while, but I think he'll be getting restless again by now.'

Andy struggled to his feet. 'Rummie?'

'This is it, Andy. Don't look so sad about it.'

Andy, trying hard to be casual, pulled a clump of grass, but couldn't seem to manage to swallow it. 'It'll be nice to have the field to myself again,' he said, chewing furiously. 'I hope everything goes well for you.'

Billy climbed over the gate. 'Red,' he called. 'Come on, feller.'

Rummie stared over the field, towards the gate. His nostrils flared and his body tensed with anticipation.

'Rummie?' said Andy.

'I've got to go now,' he replied, eyes still set upon the gate.

'Wait a minute,' said Andy. 'I just wanted to tell you, before you go . . .'

But Rummie was already cantering across the paddock. He turned as he reached the gate.

'Next year, Andy,' he cried. 'I'll see you next year.'

A few minutes later, the transporter reversed slowly down the drive and into the lane. As Jackie paused to change gear, a terrible noise echoed over the paddock.

Billy grinned. 'I guess Andy is trying to say goodbye. What a horrible grating noise donkeys make.'

In the back of the van, Rummie whinnied.

'Not as far as Red is concerned,' said Jackie. 'He's answering back as if it's music to his ears. I wonder if horses and donkeys understand each other?'

Billy shrugged his shoulders. 'That's one question you and I will never know the answer to, Jackie.'

Chapter Seventeen

IN A BLAZE OF GLORY

Summer had arrived, at last, Andy decided. He rubbed himself against the fencing posts, removing the final traces of his winter coat. The sky was high and clear and the sun was already beginning to warm the ground. It was on just such a day that Rummie had first arrived.

He thought about Rummie a lot nowadays. Would he still come back, as he had promised? Would the news make any difference? Did he still have a holiday, now that he was officially retired? Suddenly impatient, Andy trotted down to the roadside hedge. It really was most unfair. No one bothered to keep him informed about anything, and the little snippets of information that he did overhear only made him wonder all the more.

'Snap out of it,' he told himself, sternly. 'It's not like you to go around getting bothered about someone else.'

. . . Except Rummie, he thought. Rummie's different. Funny, somebody else had said that about him, too. He's my friend. I want to see him again. Perhaps if I wish, very hard, he will come.

'Rubbish, you don't believe in that sort of nonsense,' he muttered aloud. 'If he's coming, he'll come. If not, there's nothing you can do about it.'

Even so, it wasn't too much of a surprise when the orange and cream transporter turned into the drive at lunchtime. As soon as the formalities of loosing him into the field were over, Rummie and Andy raced towards each other.

'Oh, Rummie, how are you?' cried Andy, stretching up to nuzzle along the horse's neck.

For a few minutes, they stood shoulder to shoulder, nibbling each other affectionately, then Rummie turned large, moist eyes upon his friend. 'It's good to see you, old chap,' he said, gruffly. 'Good to be back again.'

'Are you all right?' asked Andy, anxiously. 'I've been so worr —.' He stopped himself. It would never do to let Rummie think he was getting soft.

'I'm fine, Andy. Fine. Let's have a quick canter and I'll show you just how fit I am.'

Andy watched with a mixture of affection and exasperation as Rummie danced off around the field. The King of Aintree had not changed one bit. He'd not been here ten minutes and he had already taken over the paddock.

As the horse galloped back towards Andy, the donkey suddenly realised that he had changed, after all. There was something defensive in the tilt of his head. This first circuit of the field wasn't being run for pure joy, like last year.

'Rummie, tell me about it,' said Andy quietly. 'Come on, you look as though you need to get things off your chest.'

Rummie stared into the far distance, while Andy waited patiently. Finally, the horse turned to his companion. 'It's taking a lot of getting used to,' he burst out. 'I'll never race again and I still can't quite believe it. I'm very busy, with all the appearances and everything, but there's nothing to aim for, any more.'

Andy looked at the great horse helplessly, wondering what he could say to comfort him. 'It had to happen, Rummie. You knew that. It couldn't carry on for ever.'

'I know, Andy – but it shouldn't have ended that way. I knew that 1978 was going to be my last National. You've no idea how much I was looking forward to it. I could have won again, I *know* I could. Why should one bruised muscle rob me of my last run?'

'How did it happen?' asked Andy.

Rummie gave a long sigh. 'Training was going along splendidly, in spite of the awful weather. The thought of Aintree was like a ray of sunshine, waiting for me at the end of that long, hard winter. This year, my training programme attracted even more attention than usual. There were reporters and cameramen to record my progress at almost every outing and I was thoroughly enjoying myself. Mr McCain was forever giving interviews outside my box and I would lean over the door, listening proudly to what he had to say.

"He's coming on really strong," he told the television reporters. "We're delighted with his performance – he's going better than ever. Needs a bit further, maybe, to get him really warmed up nowadays, but that's no problem at Aintree, as you know. I only hope the old horse can go out in a blaze of glory. That's what he deserves. If he did win – well! The main thing is, he finishes sound. That's the important thing."

Mr Stack was also in the news. He'd had a terrible setback, himself, at the beginning of the season. In the paddock at Hexham Racecourse, a horse had reared up and fallen back on to him. Among his many injuries was a badly crushed pelvis. He had to spend many long weeks in hospital, on his back. But his courage and tremendous will-power triumphed over the pain and limitations that his accident imposed and he struggled through to an incredible recovery.

Aintree was his target, too. He was determined that nothing would prevent him from riding me in my last Grand National. To think that one bruised muscle should deny us all that!

When he, too, was interviewed, he spoke of me with such genuine affection that I longed for the day when we would be reunited on the racecourse.

"The main thing is, he finishes sound," he told them. "It doesn't matter whether he wins, falls at the first fence or whatever – just that he's safe and sound at the end of the day."

There were only eight days left to go, when Billy took me out for a long work-out. That's when it happened.'

'When what happened?'

'I think it must have been a stone. I was flying along like the wind, when I suddenly felt a sharp stab of pain in my near hind foot. I continued to run, not thinking much more about it, but when we got back to the yard it had begun to stiffen up. Billy was the first to notice, and when he told Mr McCain they got my vet over straight away.

He examined my foot carefully. "This muscle is badly bruised – here, see. He probably caught a stone. How many days left to go?"

"Eight," said Mr McCain. "What are the chances?"

The vet shook his head. "It's a 'wait and see' situation, Ginger. I can't predict a thing like this – I can't tell if there's been any damage to the ligaments of his foot, you see. We'll try plenty of hot poulticing and he needs to spend lots of time in the sea – you don't need me to tell you that. Even if we do get him fit, his training programme will have been interrupted at the most vital stage, won't it? What a terrible piece of bad luck."

Mr McCain looked at Billy, helplessly. "I'll have to tell them, Billy. There are thousands of punters out there, already placing bets on him. They've a right to know."

For the rest of the week, my injury and its progress totally dominated the news. The yard was in a turmoil. The publicity I had received during the previous weeks was nothing, compared with this. Letters arrived by the sackload. The tensions increased as argument and discussion hung on the air like an invisible question mark. I could see that Mr McCain was under an enormous strain, tormented by the responsibility of a decision that *had* to wait until the eleventh hour.

I could do nothing but listen, silent and frustrated, as Billy and Mr McCain held anguished conversations in my box. For the second time in my life, I longed to be able to speak. I wanted to tell them that I could still do it, that this wasn't enough to keep me away from Aintree. It was getting better, anyway. Surely they could see that?

"He's too great to risk. If I run him and anything should happen,

I'd never forgive myself," Mr McCain said worriedly.

"Neither would the public," added Billy.

"Ginger, you're in an impossible situation," said Mrs McCain. "Even if you run him and he doesn't win, you'll be blamed, now. There he is, standing quietly in his box, perfect except for one foot that's a little bit sore, and the whole country is in an uproar about him."

That afternoon, we went down to the sands for a walk in the sea. The crowd was even larger than usual. Billy dismounted and held me still while Angela Rippon sprang up into my saddle.'

'Angela who?' asked Andy.

Rummie looked down at the donkey in amusement. 'Never mind, Andy. You wouldn't understand. Let's move on to some fresh grazing.

On Thursday afternoon, Mr McCain went off for a lengthy meeting with Mr Le Mare. As soon as he returned, he came straight to my box.

"Well?" asked Billy, anxiously.

"I've had a long discussion with the Guv'nor. He's leaving the final decision to me, but we've agreed on one thing. Whether he runs or not, this is definitely his last National. He's thirteen, Billy, though you'd never think so to look at him. It's time to retire him."

Billy stroked my muzzle. It was a sad moment for us all, but, since my foot felt so much better, I felt sure that I would be allowed my final chance to pit myself against those wicked Aintree fences.

The next morning, before dawn, we set off for the course. This was going to be my final practice gallop. We arrived there at half past six and the crowd and the cameras were already waiting for us. They filmed as I worked alongside Wot-A-Lad, another of my friends from the yard. We galloped our six furlongs at a fast pace, and finding no pain at all, my hopes soared.

By the time we got back to the yard, my wretched foot had stiffened up again. After the afternoon rest period, Billy took me once more to the sea, then, at seven o'clock that evening, the vet came again. They all watched, strangely calm now, as he examined me. He stood back and shook his head.

"If you run him, you could make it worse."

'Don't worry!' I wanted to cry. 'It doesn't matter – I'll gallop in pain, if necessary. I've done it before. I won't even feel it. Please let me have my race.'

"That's it, then," said Mr McCain, sadly. "Three and a half sound feet won't do for Aintree. I'll go and make the official announcement."

And that's what he did.

With less than twenty-four hours to go, it was announced to the world, at the end of the Nine O'Clock News, that I had retired.

Throughout that long night, I paced my box, trying to believe that it really was all over.

The first day of April dawned, grey and depressing. No wonder they call it All Fools' Day, Andy. When they got me ready and loaded me into the transporter, I was overjoyed. They had changed their minds – they were going to let me run, after all! My blood quickened with anticipation as we drew closer to the course. When Billy led me out, the crowd surged forward. The other runners were already circling the paddock and I tossed my head anxiously, looking for Mr Stack. Surely he would appear at any moment? I did not know, then, that he was already parading in the paddock on a horse called Hidden Value.

Mr McCain dashed up to us. "They won't let you ride him round," he whispered to Billy. "You'll have to lead him – the stewards say it's against the rules for him to be ridden after being declared unfit to run."

Billy began to walk me over towards the course. Behind us followed Mr McCain and a procession of pressmen and photographers. This was all wrong, I thought, as we headed back across the course towards the final run-in. I bucked uneasily and the huge crowd began to cheer and shout. Something was very wrong indeed. Why were they cheering before the race had started?

"The organisers would like to thank Mr Donald McCain and everyone connected with Red Rum, for allowing him to be paraded here today," somebody announced over the loudspeaker.

By the time I had digested this piece of information, we were approaching the stands. Like an echo of the previous year, the crowd rose to its feet and their tremendous ovation swept down to me. It was awful, Andy, hearing them shouting to me like that, when I

hadn't even run the course. As the realisation finally hit me – that this was my final, farewell journey past the Aintree Stands, I was engulfed in a wave of anger and frustration. I began to dance and buck, lashing out with my hind legs. I remember aiming one great, spirited kick towards that cheering crowd as they led me up the final run-in.

As we came up alongside the starters, who were now jostling themselves into position, one jockey turned his horse, detaching himself from the line-up, and rode towards me. I stopped bucking

Red Rum's last race – an awkward landing at Haydock in March 1978.

and waited, curiously, until they stood facing me. I looked at the horse as Mr Stack held him still, and then I raised my head towards my jockey. Our eyes met for a moment, a silent tribute between man and horse, and then Hidden Value moved restlessly, sensing something even stronger than the pre-race tension.

Mr Stack touched his riding helmet. "Goodbye, Red." He cantered back towards the line-up.

That's what they were all saying, Andy. It almost broke my heart.'

'Oh, Rummie, you mustn't feel like that. You must be the only

Red Rum receives the freedom of Southport Sands watched by his admiring public

horse, ever, to have been allowed a parade of honour like that before the Grand National. Surely that was the greatest compliment they could have paid you. You *did* end your career in a blaze of glory.'

Rummie tore at the turf angrily. 'Andy, you just don't understand. There it was, about to begin. *My* race, and for the first time in six years it was to be run without me. Try to imagine how I felt, can't you?'

'Of course I can,' said Andy gently. 'I know as well as anyone what the National means to you, but they made the right decision, you know. They couldn't have risked you, and I'm glad. So are you, if you'll just stop and think about it.'

'I would have won,' said Rummie, arrogantly.

'You can't say that. You might have won, but if you hadn't, if you'd injured yourself, just think how Mr McCain and Billy would have felt.'

Rummie looked at Andy in surprise. 'I never thought of that – but I would have won, Andy. Really.'

Andy shook his head, completely at a loss in the face of such self-assurance.

'Believe me, Andy. I'm sure of it. That's what makes it so difficult to accept. I know Aintree. I've proved myself there, over and over again. Take that fellow Pilgarlic, for instance. He's a good horse, and he finished the course. It was a very close race this time, and he was only four or five lengths behind the winner. Last year, Andy, I beat him by forty-five lengths. How do you think I felt, knowing that? It's not conceit . . .'

Andy was only half listening. He had to make Rummie pull himself together and come to terms with his life, but how? Suddenly, he could bear the tirade of bitterness no longer. 'I think you're the most ungrateful creature that ever trod pasture.'

Rummie halted in mid-sentence, staring at the donkey. 'Pardon?'

Andy repeated his remark, more confidently. A long silence followed.

Andy watched his friend closely. Then he spoke again: 'Rummie, you've always made me feel dull and rather boring, compared with you. I never really minded. You brought something new and exciting into my quiet life, but I think you need help now.

'You made it in a big way – bigger, probably, than any other horse has before, or will do again. None of your achievements is worth having if you don't end up at peace with yourself. Don't you see? You can't spend the rest of your days tormenting yourself with what might have been.

'You did it all. You've packed more into your life than most of us could ever dream of. You've been through an awful lot and you've always coped. Your future is secure and you'll always be special. What more could you possibly ask for?'

For the first time in weeks Rummie looked really happy. 'Thanks, Andy. You're right, old friend. I've been very silly, forgive me. The pressures of the last few weeks have been so unsettling – especially when that foreign gentleman came along offering half a million pounds for me. This money thing means such a lot to people, and I got quite worried.

'I should have known that they wouldn't let me down. Do you know what Mr McCain said? He said "This is his home and that's his box. That's where he lives, and that's where he'll end his days. What's money, when you're talking about Red Rum?"

'I've got everything, haven't I? My home, the family – and I'll always be able to come to you for my holidays. I've done it, Andy. No one will ever forget Red Rum.'

As Andy listened, he was determined to make sure that this holiday was going to be perfect. 'Come along, Rummie, it's almost evening. There are a couple of things I want to show you, in the top hedge.'

Suddenly calm, Rummie followed him obediently across the paddock.

Postscript

I am greatly indebted to Ivor Herbert's definitive book, *Red Rum,* which provided most of the biographical details that appear in this story.

I would like to thank Mr and Mrs McCain, Billy Beardwood and Mrs Carol Wareing for their help, advice and insight into the character of our hero.

Lastly, but by no means least, my thanks go to Rummie and Andy, for being themselves.

C.P.

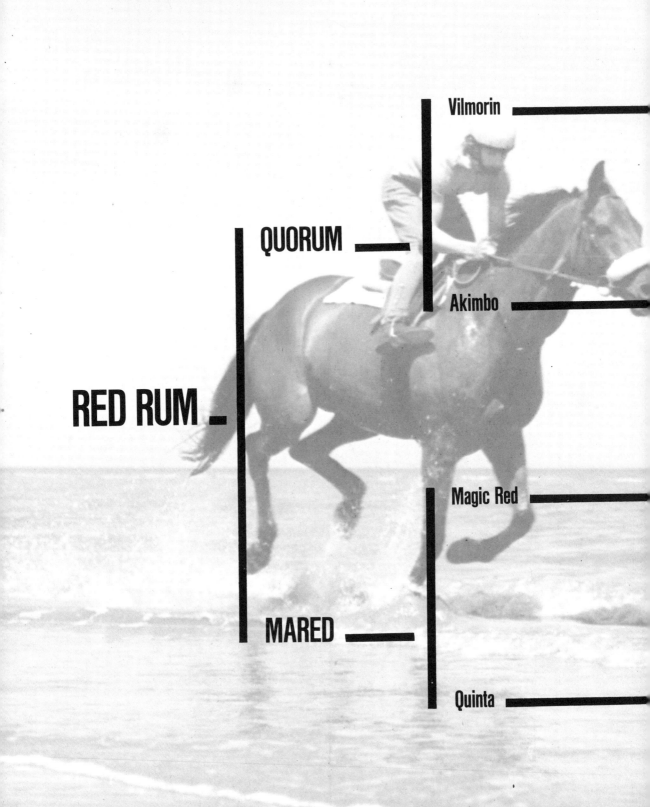

RED RUM

QUORUM

Vilmorin

Akimbo

MARED

Magic Red

Quinta